D0699064

Luke Sutton: Outrider

Luke Sutton: Outrider

LEO P. KELLEY

DOUBLEDAY & COMPANY, INC.

GARDEN CITY, NEW YORK

1984

All of the characters in this book
are fictitious, and any resemblance
to actual persons, living or dead,
except for historical personages,
is purely coincidental.

JH
Library of Congress Cataloging in Publication Data

Kelley, Leo P.
Luke Sutton, outrider.

I. Title.
PS3561.E388L86   1984   813'.54

ISBN: 0-385-18898-6
Library of Congress Catalog Card Number 83–45008

Copyright © 1984 by Leo P. Kelley
All Rights Reserved
Printed in the United States of America
First Edition

Luke Sutton: Outrider

C.1

CHAPTER 1

"Good morning, Mr. Sutton."

Luke Sutton nodded to the young man who had greeted him and wondered, as he went past him, who he was. He glanced back over his shoulder as he walked along Virginia City's Taylor Street. The man was definitely a stranger to him. But he had called him by name. He shrugged.

As Sutton walked on through the swirling clouds of smoke and alkali dust, ore wagons clattered past him. Freighters rumbled down the street. Mine whistles screeched from the flanks of Mount Davidson where clouds of steam hissed skyward and the distant rumble of operating mine machinery sounded like the grumbling of disgruntled giants.

He entered the telegraph office and picked up a pencil and printed yellow form that were lying on the counter. Without hesitation, he wrote: "Am coming home. Real anxious to see you again. Missed you all these years. Still love you." He signed it simply "Luke" and then filled in Elizabeth Dacy's name and address.

"May I be of service?" inquired the elderly telegraph operator as he stepped up to the counter.

Sutton handed him the yellow form. "How much will it set me back to send that?"

The man counted the words and then consulted a worn book. "One dollar and ten cents."

Sutton paid him and turned toward the door.

"If there's an answer," the clerk called out to him, "where can I find you and under what name, if you don't mind my asking?"

"Name's Luke Sutton. I'm staying at the International Hotel."

As he left the telegraph office, he almost collided with a pair of chattering Chinese fruit vendors who went scurrying past him with their wares slung over their shoulders. He walked slowly up sloping C Street, aware of the warm early-April sun on his body although the peaks of the Sierras off in the distance were still snow-covered.

Sutton was a rangy man, long-limbed and slender, with broad shoulders and narrow hips. His strong hands were heavily callused and his angular face had been bronzed by the sun and weathered by the wind. His nose was narrow above the thin, almost grim, line of his lips. His slightly sunken cheeks and square chin tended to catch and keep shadows which shifted as the light changed, giving him at times a menacing look although his expression didn't alter. It remained calm but alert. His gray eyes roamed the world, seeing everything, missing nothing. His straight black hair covered his ears and the nape of his neck.

He wore a pair of Frisco jeans tucked into his black jackboots and a gray flannel shirt. On his head was a black Stetson, its crown indented, its brim looped up on both sides. Tied loosely about the taut column of his neck was a blue silk bandanna and riding low on his hips was a black leather cartridge belt, all of its loops filled, its flapless holster housing his .44 Colt from which the trigger guard had been cut away.

Walking on in his typically loose-limbed fashion that was nevertheless the gait of a wary man who knows the world contains surprises, some of them highly unwelcome ones,

he soon reached the International Hotel. Once inside, he
headed for the ornate dining room which was, he discovered, nearly filled with people, mostly men, despite the
early hour.

He sat down at a small table near a window and placed
his hat on an empty chair. When a waiter materialized at
his side he waved away the menu the man offered him
and said, "A steak, rare. Two eggs, up."

The waiter left and Sutton glanced around the large
room where footfalls were muffled by the thick oriental
carpet and where conversations were muted as if in defer-
ence to the room's bright crystal chandeliers, red velvet
draperies, and richly walnut-paneled walls.

Studying the diners and the clothes they wore, he decided there was a fair sprinkling of drummers and pros-
perous local merchants among them. But some of the
early risers, despite their brocaded vests and gold watch
chains, were obviously men who had made money in the
mines. Their broken fingernails and scarred hands identi-
fied them, as did their coarse laughter and occasional
careless obscenities. But all of them—those with cheeks
reeking of bay rum and those with weather-wounded
faces—had one thing in common besides money. They
were all, Sutton noted, as sleek as house cats and as fat as
salmon in midsummer.

Sutton's steak soon came, oozing blood and flanked by
two fried eggs.

"Coffee, sir?" asked the waiter. Sutton nodded as he
began to eat.

The waiter was pouring the coffee when Sutton,
hunched over his plate, heard his name spoken. He
looked up to find William Wright, editor of Virginia City's
Territorial Enterprise, standing beside his table.

"Mind if I join you, Luke?"

Sutton, his mouth full, gestured with his knife and Wright seated himself, slapping a newspaper on the table as he did so.

"Just coffee," he told the waiter and then to Sutton he said, "I was up at Jack Penrose's house looking for you but the woman next door said you'd moved here to the hotel."

"That's right, Bill, I did after I arranged with the Wells Fargo bank to sell Jack's house and send the proceeds from the sale to his mother in England."

"It was a shame about Penrose and those other men getting themselves killed during the strike," Wright said dourly. "A damned shame."

Sutton nodded.

Wright, beaming, tapped his right index finger on the newspaper he had placed on the table. "You're front page news, Luke."

Sutton glanced inquiringly at Wright, who continued to beam as he unfolded the newspaper.

"Page one story. I wrote it myself under my pen name."

Sutton finished his breakfast, put down his knife and fork, and took the paper Wright was holding out to him.

" 'A Hero of Virginia City by Dan DeQuille,' " he read aloud.

"Catchy headline, don't you think?"

"Bill, I'm no hero and you know it," Sutton said, frowning.

"Balderdash! Why, without you that miners' strike would still be going strong, with the miners throwing beer bottles full of coal oil with blazing wicks stuck in them at the strikebreakers and at the militia that the mineowners brought to town to break the strike. There would be corpses littering both our streets and Mount Davidson had you not stepped in and talked a little sense to both sides."

"Talking sense don't make a man a hero, Bill."

"You did a great deal more than talk sense. You acted to stop the strike at a very real risk to your own life. That makes a man a hero in my book. And, I might add, in the books of just about every other citizen of our fair city." Wright paused momentarily and then remarked, "That's one of the pictures taken of you when we were down in the mine together. How do you like it?"

Sutton glanced at the picture of himself which accompanied the *Enterprise* article. "Well, there's no mistaking the fact that it's me, all right." He suddenly remembered the man, the one who had called him by name as he made his way to the telegraph office. So that's how he had known his name. He'd seen his picture in the paper.

"How does it feel to be a local hero, Luke?"

"Bill, I truly wish you would stop trying to pour me into a mold I'm not meant for. What you do is you remind me of something my pa once said and I never forgot. Now, my pa, he was a smart sort of fellow and what's more you couldn't make him believe that the brass you were trying to pass off on him was gold. He was a skeptical man, my pa was, not to mention able to think his way through a newspaper."

"What did your father say that you now remember?"

Sutton grinned. "He said, 'Paper won't refuse ink.'"

For a moment Wright's face remained impassive but then, as the meaning of Sutton's quotation struck him, his face became wreathed in a broad bright smile. He nodded enthusiastically. "Truer words were seldom spoken, Luke. And if a man needs proof all he has to do is read the advertisements the newspapers carry for Indian medicines—'cures all ailments from gout to galloping pneumonia'—or the ones for those flexible steel shirt collars some merchants in town have been selling—'comfortable as a feather bed.' Those Indian medicines are more likely to kill than cure you and those collars, if they don't choke you to death when you turn your head suddenly to stare at a pretty woman, they most certainly will chafe you until your neck turns raw."

"Paper won't refuse ink," Sutton repeated, still grinning.

Wright laughed and then asked, "What are your plans, Luke? Will you be staying on here in Virginia City?"

"To answer your second question first, Bill, no, I'm heading home."

"To Texas?"

"To Texas. And, as for your first question, *whoooeee,* do I have me some plans! Fine ones they are too. I'm fixing to get myself married, first off, and then to start in on raising a family. It's something I had to put off doing for quite a spell."

"Because you felt you had to hunt down the four men who killed your brother."

"Now that I've gone and done that, I'm free to live my life the way I want to live it and that way means marrying a fine figure of a woman named Elizabeth Dacy who I had to leave behind me when I set out after those killers three —nearly four—years ago.

"I can't wait to see her again, Bill," Sutton continued, leaning back in his chair, his voice becoming dreamy. "She's a sight that'd make a lame man dance a jig and a hearty one throw a conniption fit. She's got herself a real sweet voice and skin softer than fresh-churned butter. She's got a way of walking that makes a man like me feel faint just watching her and a way of talking soft and low that more than once has set my blood to boiling."

"It's clear to me that you're in love with this Miss Dacy. Is she in love with you?"

"Sure she is," Sutton replied confidently. "We'd planned on getting married, the two of us, before I set out after my brother's killers." Sutton paused thoughtfully for a moment. "I just now sent her word by telegraph that I was finally coming home."

"We'll be sorry to see you leave Virginia City, Luke. You have been and could continue to be an asset to our town."

"It's real nice of you to say such a thing, Bill, and I wouldn't mind one bit staying on here were it not for the fact that I've a yearning to go home where I belong and where Elizabeth's been waiting on me nigh onto four years now."

"I can understand your feelings," Wright commented. "A man tends to wither if he's cut off from his roots for too long a time. Such a state can turn a man sour."

Sutton heard the note of wistfulness in Wright's voice. "Seeing as how you've been a Washoe widower for so long, Bill, I reckon you know what you're talking about. Though you haven't turned sour nor withered so far as I can tell."

"But it's no good being separated from the ones you love—in my case, from my wife and family. It's the lure of the Lode, Luke, damn the donkey if it isn't! The Comstock got to me almost the instant I arrived here and it's still got a hard hold on me. But someday . . ."

As Wright's words trailed away, Sutton said, "Someday you'll go home." Wright nodded absently, lost in thought. "Like I'm going to do tomorrow," Sutton added. "And that said, I'd best be about the doing of it." He rose, clapped his hat on his head, and held out his hand.

Wright stood up and shook it. "Take good care of yourself, Luke. It's been a pleasure knowing you."

"Same here, Bill." Sutton left the table, paid the cashier for his breakfast, and went out into the lobby where small palms in china pots waved in the breeze that was wafting through the open front door of the hotel.

He was about to step into the hydraulic elevator when he heard his name called. He turned to find the woman who had called out to him hurrying across the lobby.

He studied her as she came toward him. Plain. Worried, judging by the tight expression she's got on her face. Maybe a little afraid too. Her eyes look kind of anxious.

"Mr. Sutton, I'm awfully sorry to bother you and I hope you don't mind my doing so, but it's very important to me and I simply did not know where else to turn, so I inquired as to your whereabouts and was told that you were living here in the hotel, and I came here and went to your room but there was no answer to my knock, so I came down to the lobby to wait for you and—"

Sutton took her arm. "Why don't you slow down some so's you can catch your breath? Then you can speak your piece." He steered her to the nearest cluster of high-backed leather chairs and eased her into one before seating himself beside her. "Now, then. Tell me what it is you want with me."

"Thank you, Mr. Sutton. Oh, thank you so very much. I knew you would be kind. I just knew it. But I was still hesitant about approaching you even though the story about you in the *Enterprise*—"

Sutton frowned.

"—said that you were a gentleman . . ."

Paper won't refuse ink. The words echoed in Sutton's mind.

". . . and that you had done so much to help the miners win their battle with the mineowners. So I said to myself that I must talk to you about . . ." The woman lowered her eyes to her hands which were tightly clutching her reticule.

"Talk to me about what, ma'am?"

The woman looked up at Sutton and said, "My name is Edith Soames and I live here in Virginia City at Number 41 C Street. I was widowed last year. My man—the mine he was working in—a tunnel collapsed. Maybe that's why I want my brother found. Since Bob died, I've been so lonely and I have no other kin. Just my brother Vernon. If he's still alive. Oh, Mr. Sutton, will you try to find Vernon for me? You will try, won't you?"

"Mrs. Soames, ma'am, I can't. I'm heading home to Texas tomorrow and—"

"I can pay you for your services," Mrs. Soames interrupted and quickly opened her reticule. She withdrew an envelope and held it out to Sutton. "There are five hundred dollars in this envelope, Mr. Sutton. The money is yours if you'll try to find Vernon for me."

Sutton ignored the envelope Mrs. Soames was holding out to him in a hand that trembled faintly. "Mrs. Soames, I haven't the slightest notion why you came to me or why you want me to hunt for your brother, whoever he is and wherever he might be for whatever reason."

"I came because, after I read about how you spent so much time tracking the men who killed your brother all over creation, I knew you were a man of action, a man who wouldn't rest until he had accomplished any task he set for himself, a man of courage and no little ingenuity."

"You oughtn't to believe everything you read in the newspapers, Mrs. Soames."

"It's untrue what Dan DeQuille wrote about you?" Mrs. Soames rummaged about again in her reticule and this time withdrew a folded piece of paper which she handed to Sutton.

He took it, unfolded it, and read Wright's article. "I guess what it says here is true enough, by and large."

"Will you help me, Mr. Sutton?"

"Mrs. Soames, I've been away from home and the woman I love for nearly four years now. I want to go back where I was born and brung up. I want to marry the woman who's been waiting on me all this time. Maybe you can understand how I feel."

Mrs. Soames pressed her lips together and then nodded slightly. "I understand. To be away from the one you love is a painful experience. When Bob was killed in the mine last year—as the days passed I got to missing him more and more. When you've been married to a man like Bob Soames as I was for so many years—and had no children—two people like us grow very close and then, when one is gone, the other—the other suffers so. Yes, Mr. Sutton, I can understand why you want to return to the woman you love and had to leave. Please forgive me for bothering you."

As Mrs. Soames got to her feet, so did Sutton.

"I want to wish you the very best, you and your fiancée," she said. "I'm sure you'll both be very happy. Thank you for your time, Mr. Sutton."

Sutton watched Mrs. Soames walk through the lobby and then out the door to disappear in the crowd outside. He stood staring after her for a moment and then turned back and made his way to the elevator.

Once inside his room on the fourth floor, he dropped his hat on the marble-topped dresser, bent down, and pulled the canvas carpetbag he had bought the day before out from under the bed. Placing it on the bed, he opened a drawer of the dresser, took out the clothes it contained, and placed them inside the carpetbag.

When he had finished packing his meager belongings, he went to the window and drew back the Nottingham lace curtain. Staring down at the sprawling city that had

been spawned by the discovery of silver, he felt excitement surge within him because of thoughts of Elizabeth
Dacy which were whirling through his mind, a joyous mix
of memory and anticipation, a blending of moments lived
with those promised.

He watched a man and a woman, her arm linked in his,
hurry along the street across from the hotel. He saw not
the man and woman but himself and Elizabeth Dacy.
When the man darted a glance behind him and then
quickly kissed the woman's cheek, Sutton smiled.

But his smile vanished at the sound of someone knock-
ing on his door. His hand automatically gripped the butt
of his revolver as he swiftly turned from the window,
letting the curtain fall, and crossed the room. He opened
the door and the boy standing outside in the hall started to
speak but then stopped, his startled eyes on Sutton's hand
which was still on his gun butt.

Sutton removed his hand from his revolver. "You want
me?"

"You're Mr. Luke Sutton?" the boy inquired uneasily.

"I am."

The boy thrust a folded piece of paper into Sutton's
hand before hurrying away down the hall.

Sutton closed the door, unfolded the paper, and, leaning back against the door, read the telegraph message the
boy had delivered to him, his body stiffening as he did so,
his mind numbing.

When he had finished reading it, he angrily balled the
paper in one hand and hurled it across the room.

It hit the wall and fell to the floor.

Sutton went over to the bed and flopped down on his
back upon it, his hands clasped behind his head, his eyes
on the ceiling he did not see above him as the words he
had just read resounded in his mind and rage rose within

him—a red rage that was directed at the world which could turn and turn so sharply that a man's life was abruptly upended, a rage that was directed as well at the woman in that world who had caused it to lurch so suddenly and bring an end to his happiness and death to his dreams.

No!

The fruitless denial roared in his mind.

He suddenly got up from the bed, picked up the message, and read it again, hoping he had misunderstood it somehow, hoping he had made some sort of mistake . . .

NO WORD FROM YOU IN ALMOST FOUR YEARS. AM MARRIED NOW. HAVE DAUGHTER TEN MONTHS OLD. NEVER KNEW IF YOU WERE ALIVE OR DEAD ALL THIS TIME. YOUR HOMEPLACE SOLD FOR UNPAID TAXES.

It was signed "Mrs. Elizabeth Montague."

He had made no mistake. He had not misunderstood the message.

She wasn't Elizabeth Dacy anymore. She was Mrs. Elizabeth Montague now. A wife. A mother. And she was lost to him because she had been found in his absence by a man named Montague.

His rage intensified. He tried to make himself hate her. He returned to the bed, flopped down upon it again, and knew—and hated the knowing—that he had loved so deeply, almost desperately.

There was no escaping that fact. He had not ever contacted her during the years he had hunted down his brother Dan's killers. She had been part—the most important part—of a life he had deliberately put behind him the day he had set out to seek vengeance.

His life—the one he had left behind him—had seemed

dead to him during those long years as he rode relentlessly on, hunting, always hunting, the hunt a fever in his blood and a malaise in his mind. He was well aware of the fact that he had been a prisoner during those years, a prisoner of four murdering men, and it was not until the last of them was dead, a death that had occurred only days ago, that the door of his prison had swung open and left him a free man, free he had believed—naïvely believed, he now knew—to return to the world he had left so long ago and begin living in it again as if those years had not existed, as if nothing had changed, as if the world, frozen in space and time, had hung motionless, only waiting for him to enter it again, thaw it, and make it move once more.

You've won, he thought bitterly. Dead all four of you may be, he thought, but you've won a victory over me from your graves. You've robbed me of the woman I loved. You've looted my life.

No, he thought, his fists clenching at his sides. *No, dammit!* Those four men who killed Dan aren't to blame for what happened, he told himself. The blame was his, he realized. He could have—should have—gotten in touch with Elizabeth from time to time. She was not to blame for having married another man during his long and silent absence.

Your homeplace sold for unpaid taxes.

Another direct result of his overwhelming obsession with vengeance. He knew it. He could not deny it. Elizabeth was gone. So was the homeplace.

Sutton suddenly felt himself foundering. Unmoored and unanchored, he felt the unstable and tumultuous sea beneath him swell and shift and for a brief instant he thought he was going to drown.

But some time later the bitterness within him began to

subside and he lay motionless on the bed as he silently accepted the sad requiem he heard whispering within him for the loss of a world and a time and a woman that had all once been his but were his no more.

Time passed and he continued to lie without moving on the bed as the sun rose higher in the sky and then began to descend. The solemn requiem faded, finally died, and he came to know that in endings are born beginnings.

He got up from the bed, put on his hat, and left his room and then the hotel.

Minutes later, he was standing in front of the house with the iron and brick facade that was Number 41 C Street. He knocked on the door.

He didn't have to knock a second time. As Mrs. Soames opened the door, he said, "You still want to pay me five hundred dollars to find your brother?"

Mrs. Soames, flustered, nodded instead of speaking.

"Can I come in?"

"Yes, of course. Please do, Mr. Sutton."

He looked around the neat parlor, modestly furnished, and seated himself in an upholstered wing chair as Mrs. Soames, murmuring something about the deepening darkness outside, lit a coal-oil lamp and placed it on the table near where Sutton was sitting.

As she seated herself across from him, he said, "Tell me about your brother. You said his name was Vernon, as I recall." He saw the question evident in Mrs. Soames's eyes and to keep her from asking it, inquired, "How old's Vernon?"

"He'd be twenty-seven now—if he's still alive. His last name is Adams, which was my maiden name."

"When did you last see him?"

"Twenty years ago."

"Twenty years ago!" Sutton hated the harshness he

heard in his voice. When he spoke again his voice was more modulated, almost gentle. "Where?"

"Where?"

"Where'd you last see him?"

"It was along the Gila River. Near a little town called Dead Horse in Arizona Territory." Mrs. Soames began to bite her lower lip, her head lowering.

But Sutton had seen the tears gleaming in her eyes.

"We were traveling west," Mrs. Soames said, her voice little more than a sigh, "the six of us. My mother, my father, my mother's parents, Vernon, and me. We had passed through Dead Horse—a funny name for a town, isn't it?" She tried a smile that didn't work. "We had bought provisions—lots of flour, I remember, because both Vernon and I did so love the biscuits my mother used to bake. Vernon had the terrible habit of stuffing himself with those biscuits until a body would think he'd surely burst. He was only seven then but could eat biscuits until the cows came home."

"What happened west of Dead Horse?"

"Apaches."

The word hung in the air between Sutton and Mrs. Soames and seemed to tick there, an ominous metronome.

"Apaches," Sutton prompted moments later when Mrs. Soames, obviously trapped in the claws of ugly memories, said no more.

She looked up at him, the tears in her eyes glistening but her jaw set and her narrow shoulders rigid. "They were all killed that day—all but Vernon and me. I hid in the hollow of a rotting deadfall and I heard the whooping of the Apaches. I saw the knives—bright steel at first—and then red. I heard my mother scream. She never stopped screaming all the time those savages—used her before eventually killing her. I held both of my hands over my mouth to keep myself from screaming. I saw first my grandparents and then my father butchered. Finally, my mother."

Mrs. Soames's body seemed to shrink in upon itself, seemed to dissolve as if the bones within it were melting. She huddled in her chair, her arms clasped about her body, shuddering, small tortured sounds slipping from between her lips.

Sutton said nothing.

"I saw them," she continued some time later, "take Vernon. He had been standing there in the midst of all the awful noise near our Conestoga wagon that the Apaches had set afire, not moving, not speaking—just standing there as if he were deep in a dream with his eyes wide open. An Apache seized him by the hair and pulled him up and threw him over his pony's neck. Even then Vernon didn't cry out. He didn't move. And then, moments later, they were all gone. I couldn't see or hear any of them anymore.

"I stayed in the hollow of the deadfall all that day and through the night, thinking *They'll come back—they'll come back because they didn't catch me and when they realize that I got away they'll come back and they'll* . . .

"I don't think I moved a muscle during all those hours. I kept my eyes shut. I kept my hands over my mouth. I listened. The wind stirred the branches but the sounds I heard weren't branches rubbing together—not for me. They were Apaches coming back for me.

"Next day a man found me. He was searching for kindling. I fled from him but he chased and caught me. I wouldn't—I couldn't—speak to him. Or to anyone. Not for days. The man was part of a family that was traveling to Oregon. They buried my folks and took me with them.

It was September by the time we reached the settlement that became Virginia City and it was already snowing in the Sierras. They decided to wait for spring before continuing their journey.

"In the end, we all remained here. I lived with the Soames family and later I married their son, Bob. I never saw Vernon again and never had word of him or learned what happened to him. Now, with Bob dead and gone—well, I want so badly to see Vernon, to be with him again. Oh, I did try to find him when I got older. I put advertisements in newspapers. I even journeyed once to Arizona Territory and talked to a major in the cavalry about Vernon, but he knew nothing and couldn't help me.

"I'm alone now, Mr. Sutton, and I don't know how much longer I might live. I don't want to die without trying once more to find Vernon. That's why I came to you. I'm so glad that you've come here to see me this evening."

"Mrs. Soames, first off let me say I'm sorry for all your trouble. But I've got to tell you the truth. Your brother's trail's grown cold as a sinner's conscience by now. Vernon —were I to find him—and I got to say frankly my chances of doing that seem to me to be mighty slim—well, there's something you ought to consider."

"What is it?"

"White children raised by Apaches—or any other tribe of Indians for that matter—don't always take kindly to being brought back to live with whites. Oh, some do, sure. But a whole lot don't. Then there's the fact that even if they do come back, their friends and folks might not like their ways of doing and thinking things. Indian captivity makes a mark on a man or woman, one that's not always easy to rub out. You might not like what Vernon is today.

He's a man now and not the little biscuit-eating boy you remember anymore."

"I appreciate your telling me that. I have thought about it and I know what you say is so. But I feel I have to know what happened to Vernon. If he's alive, I want to see him again, no matter what he might have become. It's a deep yearning I have inside me and it's become, since my husband passed away, as much a part of me as my blood or bones."

"Vernon might be dead."

Mrs. Soames nodded.

"I might not be able to find him."

Mrs. Soames rose from her chair and left the room. When she returned, she was carrying the envelope she had earlier offered to Sutton. "The money," she said. "It's yours. For *trying* to find Vernon. All I ask is that you return and tell me if you succeeded—or failed—in your mission."

"It might be best if I took just a part of the money to start with. You could pay me the rest once I get back and tell you what I found out—if I find out anything."

"Mr. Sutton, I've known many men in my time and I am not an unintelligent or insensitive woman. I've known good men and I've known bad. I've known men I would trust with my life and men I wouldn't trust to draw water from a well. Take the money, Mr. Sutton. All of it."

Sutton took the envelope from Mrs. Soames. "I'll do my best to find out whatever I can about your brother, Mrs. Soames. Would you by any chance happen to have a picture of him?"

"No, I'm afraid not. We were poor folks in those days, Mr. Sutton, and we had no money to spare for what my mother would have called folderols."

"Don't matter all that much. If he's ali—if I find him, I

most likely wouldn't be able to recognize him from a picture somebody took of him when he was but seven and him now a whole lot older than that."

"I can tell you that he had brown hair but I confess that I can't remember the color of his eyes."

"Maybe I'll find him, if I'm lucky."

"A man like you doesn't depend on luck, Mr. Sutton. If Vernon is to be found, I believe you are the man to find him."

Sutton pocketed the envelope and started for the door. Before he reached it, Mrs. Soames spoke his name and he turned back to face her.

"You're not going home to Texas and your fiancée then?"

"Nope."

Mrs. Soames hesitated a moment and then said, "I shan't ask what made you change your mind because I'm certain that whatever it was was not a happy event. But I am glad that you decided to search for Vernon. It's sad but true that one person's misfortune can be another's bonanza."

Sutton nodded and then turned and went out the door into the young night that held Virginia City in its dark embrace, imagining bloodthirsty Apaches stalking in the shadows that lurked just beyond the pools of light that were being spilled by the gas lamps flickering high above him on their iron stanchions.

CHAPTER 2

Nearly two weeks had passed since Sutton had agreed to search for Vernon Adams and now, as he rode into Callville, Nevada, which sprawled along the bank of the Colorado River, he was happy to have left behind him the trail's solitary days and long lonely nights.

Around him as he slowly rode the bay down the wide main street of the bustling river town were countless people entering and leaving shops and equally countless wagons of all kinds loaded with freight which threatened at any moment to completely clog the street as they made their noisy way from warehouses to docks before returning empty for another load of merchandise destined to be steamboated down the Colorado River which flowed past numerous thriving towns as it made its way south to the Gulf of California.

"I said bankrupt, gentlemen, and that is exactly what I meant," boomed a coatless and gaudily gallused man wearing a derby hat, who was standing atop a wooden platform under a sign reading BAILEY'S WHOLESALE DRY GOODS.

"Bailey, I repeat, has gone bankrupt and his misfortune is your chance to profit at this auction I'm about to conduct of his goods which have been impounded and ordered sold by the court bailiff. Let us begin, gentlemen. I have here a crate of the finest muslin and I ask you, gentlemen, what am I bid for it? Do I hear twenty dollars, twenty dollars—*ten?* Why, sir, the cloth in this crate is worth twice twenty dollars, but I'll take your ten-dollar bid as a floor bid, and now, as for the rest of you enterprising gentlemen, do I hear fifteen . . ."

Sutton was barely conscious of the auctioneer's raucous exhortations as his gaze roamed from one false-fronted wooden building to the next on both sides of the street. When he finally spotted a livery stable, he rode toward it. He slid out of the saddle and, gripping the bay's reins, led the horse inside where he found a farrier busy building a fire in his forge.

"I'd like some grain for my horse," he told the sweating man. "Some oats. Mix in some barley and a little corn. I want him rubbed down real good and watered well."

The farrier nodded in the direction of an empty stall and Sutton led the bay into it. He removed his gear from the animal and hung it on one of the stall's wooden walls.

As he started toward the door of the livery, the farrier called out, "How long you figure on leaving him?"

"How long'll it take for you to see to him?"

"An hour, I reckon."

"I'll be back in an hour."

After leaving the livery, he made his way to the barbershop across the street where he bathed in the back room. Then he had his face shaved and his hair cut by the garrulous barber who eagerly informed him that Callville was growing "by leaps and bounds" and declared the town to be "a blossoming and booming metropolis," receiving from Sutton noncomittal grunts by way of response.

As the barber, with a flourish, whipped away the striped cloth and the bootblack finished buffing Sutton's now gleaming black boots, Sutton rose from the chair, paid both men, and asked, "Where might I be liable to find the steamboat agent?"

"The Colorado Steam Navigation Company has their office right smack on the waterfront. Their name's on their window. You can't miss it."

"Much obliged." Once outside the barbershop, Sutton made his way to the waterfront where he quickly located the office he had been seeking and entered it.

"Good day to you, sir," said the rotund man who rose from a chair behind the counter. "May I be of some service?"

"When's the next steamboat set to head down south to Yuma?"

The man behind the counter withdrew a gold watch from his rumpled vest pocket, snapped it open, glanced at it, and said, "The *Mojave II* is due to dock at Callville at noon today."

"That'll suit me just fine."

As Sutton reached into his pocket and withdrew his money, the agent said, "You'll be wanting a stateroom, I take it. The *Mojave II* has fine accommodations on board and the meals served are—"

"No stateroom. That's a bit too fancified for me. I'll take deck passage to Yuma—for me and my horse."

"Staterooms *are* rather expensive," the agent commented, eyeing the wad of bills in Sutton's hand. "But well worth it, especially for someone traveling as far as Yuma. Carpeted floors, feather beds—"

"What you're staring at," Sutton said, indicating the money he was holding in his hand, "may have to last me a good long time. I don't intend to spend any more of it than I have to right now so's it'll be likely to last me. I'll bed down on deck."

"As you wish, sir. Do you have any baggage?"

"Nope. Just my horse."

The agent made out a ticket and handed it to Sutton. "That will be forty-eight dollars."

Sutton paid the man. As he was about to leave the office, the ticket agent called out, "I hope you will have a pleasant journey, sir."

Once outside, Sutton made his way back to the livery stable where he found the farrier currying his bay. As the farrier completed his task, Sutton unfolded his saddle blanket and shook it out.

Then, after paying the farrier, he saddled and bridled the bay and led it out of the livery.

He withdrew the remainder of his money from his jeans pocket and, in one swift surreptitious movement, shoved his wad of bills deep into his right boot where it rested snugly just above his ankle. Then he swung into the saddle, turned the bay, and rode down the main street toward the river which lay glistening in the distance beneath the sun that was growing hotter as the day grew older.

When he reached the docks, he found the twin-stacked *Mojave II,* a stern-wheeler, already moored and its passengers disembarking. He sat his horse and watched as freight was unloaded from the boat's cargo deck by shirtless and straining stevedores who piled it up in no apparent order on the dock.

Twenty minutes later, the process Sutton had observed reversed itself. Now, passengers boarded the boat and cargo was piled on the deck that had been partially cleared only minutes before. Teamsters drove wagons up the staging to take their places in the large open shed that almost completely covered the main deck. Several head of cattle went lowing up the staging and into the shed. They were followed by men carring heavy sacks, bulky bales, boxes of all sizes, and scores of barrels. A team of

stevedores pushing wheelbarrows piled high with cord-
wood plodded up the staging and then headed for the
forward housing to dump their loads that would soon feed
the flames inside the fireboxes of the boilers which, along
with the engines, were sheltered in the housing.

At the stern of the boat, several deckhands were busily
engaged in securing the line attached to a barge, loaded
with mining machinery, riding low in the ruddy river
water some distance from the huge paddle wheel.

"All aboard!" shouted a deckhand and Sutton dismounted and led his horse up the staging onto the main
deck where he handed his ticket to the steward standing
by the rail.

As the staging was being withdrawn from the boat by
men on the bank, Sutton located an empty spot on the
main deck and wrapped the reins of his bay around a
latticed fence that bordered one side of the warehouse-
like shed.

He seated himself on the deck with his back braced
against the low fence, his forearms propped on his knees.

"Where are you headed, mister?" asked a young man
near him who was struggling with the lashings on his
cargo which rested in a flatbed wagon.

"Yuma. Down in Arizona Territory," Sutton answered.

"I'm headed for Hardyville myself," the man volunteered. "Got me a right nice little general store there, me
and the missus. It gives us a comfortable livelihood, I'm
happy to say. Good thing too, considering we'll be three to
feed in two more months or so, according to the doc." The
man beamed proudly at Sutton.

"You're a lucky man," Sutton told him and thought of
Elizabeth and then of the homeplace he had also lost.

"That's a fact," the man crowed, and then, "Dammit all
to hell and Hattiesburg!"

Sutton got up and went over to the man. "Let me have hold of that."

"These ropes keep slipping on me," the man muttered.

"That's on account of you've gone and tied yourself a granny knot in these two rope ends. Granny knots now, they just won't hold. What you got to do is like this."

Sutton untied the granny knot, slid the right rope under the left rope and brought it around until the ends of both ropes pointed upward.

"Now then," he said as the man watched him. "What you got to do is you got to bring this right end—it was the left end before—over the other end, down under and around like this, and then tighten up on it. Reckon that'll hold your goods in place even if we hit a storm that stirs up the water some on the way south."

"Much obliged. By the way, my name's Jim Collins."

"Luke Sutton. Glad to know you, Collins." Sutton took Collins' outstretched hand and shook it.

He was surprised at how easily he had given his real name to Collins and with only the faintest sense of apprehension. It's been a long time, he thought, since I've been so free and open about naming myself out loud to a stranger. But I can be open about it now. Now that I'm no longer a wanted man.

"You married, Sutton?"

Sutton looked away from Collins and shook his head. "Expected to be. But I'm not, as it turns out."

Collins made a comment but it was drowned out by the blast of a whistle.

Sutton, as the boilers began to hiss and rumble and the boat pulled away from the dock, got up and walked forward to stand staring downriver, aware of the wind that was rising and whirling southward. A moment later, he turned and climbed the stairs to the texas deck where he made his way past a row of cabin doors. He climbed more stairs and emerged on the boat's hurricane deck. Then he climbed the narrow ladder to the pilothouse which was perched above the texas where the boat's officers were housed. He found the captain inside the pilothouse talking to the pilot.

"I'm sorry," the captain said to Sutton, "but passengers are not allowed in here."

"Just want to ask you a question, Captain," Sutton said.

"Well?"

"About what time do you figure we'll get to Yuma?"

"Well," began the captain thoughtfully, "we're scheduled to arrive at Yuma at noon tomorrow. However, we have a stop to make at Hardyville first and the loading and unloading of freight does not always go as smoothly as we all would like, so our schedule may be disrupted."

"Much obliged, Captain." Sutton left the pilothouse and after climbing down the ladder to the cabin deck, he entered the Gentlemen's Cabin where he found a number of well-dressed men sitting and standing about as a white-coated waiter moved among them serving drinks. At the opposite end of the Gentlemen's Cabin, Sutton noticed the closed folding door which he knew led to the Ladies' Cabin.

As the waiter was about to pass him, Sutton stepped in front of him. "What does a man have to do to get himself some whiskey?"

"I'll fill your order in a moment, sir. Excuse me."

The waiter, balancing a tray on which several filled glasses rested, moved on among the passengers but returned within minutes and handed Sutton a glass partially filled with whiskey.

Sutton paid the price the waiter named and added a tip.

He stood just inside the door of the Gentlemen's Cabin,

leaning against the wall and sipping the whiskey. He watched as a folding table was put in place by another waiter and three men promptly seated themselves at it.

Moments later, a waiter brought a sealed pack of cards, and moments after that, a silent, almost solemn game of poker was in progress at the table.

The door beside Sutton opened and a woman entered the cabin, followed by a tall man Sutton found notable for the cold cast of his eyes and the way his fingers constantly flexed, almost imperceptibly, as if he were about to seize something or someone.

Sutton noticed the poker players pause and boldly appraise the woman who had preceded the ice-eyed man as she made her way to the small bar and murmured something to the man behind it.

If she knows she's out of place, Sutton thought, she don't seem to mind one little bit. Maybe she's got no use for etiquette of the kind that would properly confine her to the Ladies' Cabin down there behind that folding door.

The woman turned from the bar with a small cordial glass held daintily in her right hand, the green liquid in the glass glistening in the light of the fancily engraved lamps that lit the cabin, seemingly unaware of the stares of the men and apparently unbothered by the thick clouds of cigar smoke drifting in the still air.

The man who had entered the cabin with her was paying no attention to her as he shook hands with the three men at the poker table and then sat down to join them.

Sutton thumbed his hat back on his head and watched the woman as a man near her coughed and then spat into the brass cuspidor near her feet. She sipped delicately from her glass, oblivious of the man's action.

The door opened again and Sutton turned as Collins

entered the cabin and said, "Sutton, let me buy you a drink."

Sutton held up his glass. "Got one, but thanks just the same."

"I'll go get me one and be right back," Collins said and hurried across the cabin to the bar. When he returned, he grinned and said, "I splurged. The best French brandy." He held out his glass to Sutton. "To a bright today and a brighter tomorrow."

Sutton touched his glass to Collins' and then both men drank.

"Come on," Collins urged, taking Sutton by the arm. "Let's go see if we can sit in on that poker game over there and have a go at wooing Lady Luck."

Sutton drained his glass, placed it on a table, and let himself be led to the poker table.

Minutes later, as one of the men gathered up the cards and prepared to deal, Collins said, "Excuse me, gents. I'm Jim Collins and this here's a friend of mine named Luke Sutton. Mind if we sit in?"

The men at the table looked up at Collins. All, that is, except the man with the uneasy fingers who was staring coldly up at Sutton.

"You go ahead if you've a mind to play," Sutton told Collins. "I'll just watch, if that's all right with you gents."

"I'll be back directly," said the man who had been staring at Sutton. "I need a drink."

Collins sat down at the table and the poker players introduced themselves to him.

"I'm Gil Ellison," announced the man who had briefly left the table as he returned. He shook hands with Collins, ignoring Sutton. As he sat down, the poker game resumed and Ellison began to win pot after pot to the obvious chagrin of the other players, most especially Collins. After twenty more minutes of play during which he lost a considerable amount of money, he gave a groan and then a despairing glance in Sutton's direction before rising and telling Ellison and the others that he had had enough.

"More than enough," he amended. "I'm just about cleaned out. Come on, Sutton. I've got just about enough left to buy you that drink now if you'll have one on me."

"Save your money, Collins," Sutton suggested.

But Collins insisted, so Sutton followed him to the bar, keenly conscious of the woman who had entered the cabin with Ellison and who was now seated at a table next to the bar.

"What'll you have, Sutton?" Collins inquired.

"Whiskey'll be fine."

"Two whiskeys," Collins told the bar dog and then, casting a doleful glance in Sutton's direction added, "No more French brandy for me. Not this trip anyway. Not after that fast and furious game I was just in."

"Maybe you shouldn't play with professionals," Sutton remarked.

"All of us lost a lot. Except Gil Ellison. What do you mean 'professionals'?"

"I mean Ellison. He's a riverboat gambler."

"How do you know that?"

"He's wearing a pair of miniature dice on his watch chain which tells the world what he wants it to know about him."

Collins turned to stare at Ellison. "I never did notice those dice. Do you think he cheated?"

"Couldn't say. It's possible. Maybe even likely. He—"

"*Oohhh!*"

The exclamation was soft, almost plaintive, and at the sound of it, Sutton stopped speaking and turned to his right. He quickly put down his glass and moved to the table at which the woman who was Ellison's companion had been sitting.

She was on her feet now but swaying slightly. Her right hand rested on the table and her torso was bent over it as, with her left hand, she clutched at her throat.

When Sutton reached her, he put one arm around her waist and then thrust out one booted foot and pulled her chair toward him. "You'd best sit down," he advised the woman. "What's wrong?"

As he helped her into the chair, she shook her head dazedly. She drew a deep breath and weakly fanned the air in front of her face with one hand. "Smoke," she whispered, the word little more than a sigh. "It's so smoky in here. It's hard to breathe."

"You think maybe you can make it out onto the deck?" Sutton asked her. "You can lean on me. The fresh air ought to help straighten you out."

"Yes, I do believe that's what I need. Fresh air. I feel quite faint actually." She rose unsteadily to her feet. "May I?"

She slipped her arm into Sutton's and they made their way out of the cabin and onto the deck.

"Oh, this is ever so much better," she declared brightly. "I do thank you, Mr. Sutton. You're very kind."

"You know my name?"

"Of course I do. I heard your friend Mr. Collins mention it when he introduced himself and you to Mr. Ellison and the others. I'm Miss Laureen Driscoll."

"Glad to make your acquaintance Miss Driscoll."

"Are you traveling far, Mr. Sutton?"

"To Yuma."

"On business?"

"You might say that."

"I note that you travel armed." Laureen's eyes dropped

to Sutton's holstered Colt that rested against his right hip. "Are you in a dangerous business, Mr. Sutton?" she inquired coyly as she looked up at him again.

"Just living can be a dangerous business," he said after a moment, noticing that her eyes were twinkling as she studied him, her hands folded demurely in front of her.

"You look like a man who could handle himself quite well were he to be faced with sudden danger."

"I manage. But I'm not faced with danger at the moment." Sutton's eyes narrowed and a grin ghosted across his face. "Or am I?"

Laureen affected a shocked expression. "Dangerous? Me? Why, Mr. Sutton, I'm disposed to faint at the sight of lightning and shudder at the sound of thunder."

"But Mr. Ellison, he looks after you, I reckon. Keeps you safe and sound."

"We're friends, Gil and I, if that's what you mean."

Sutton heard the suddenly sharp edge to Laureen's tone. "Mr. Ellison now, he's one real lucky man to have so lovely a looking friend as yourself."

Laureen's face softened. She smiled coquettishly up at Sutton. "What a nice compliment to pay a lady. I thank you for it, sir."

Sutton was about to speak when Laureen's face suddenly assumed a stricken expression and she began to crumple. He reached out and caught her in both of his arms. "You sick, Miss Driscoll?"

"I don't know—I'm—so silly—sorry to be such a bother to you. Oh, I really must sit down—lie down. My stateroom . . . Mr. Sutton, could you—would you—"

Sutton bent down and placed Laureen's right arm over his shoulder and then, with his left arm around her waist, he asked, "Where's your stateroom?"

"On the other side of the boat. It's the 'California'."

"We'll go slow," Sutton said and they did, as they made their way along the deck and then around the forward end of the boat, Sutton silent, Laureen breathing shallowly, to the second door in the long line of doors, the one which bore the name "California."

"It's unlocked," Laureen managed to murmur and Sutton reached out and opened the door.

As he entered the cabin, his eyes on the bed covered with a damask spread, Laureen's arm slipped from his shoulder. He was about to turn toward her, his arm tightening on her waist, when she suddenly drew away from him, stepping briskly backward.

"Hold it right there, Sutton!"

Sutton, his eyes on the other door opposite him beyond the bed, went rigid as he felt a gun barrel press against the small of his back. Slowly, he raised his arms above his head.

"It's just a derringer I'm holding on you," said the familiar male voice from behind Sutton. "But one sure shot's enough to maybe split your spine in two."

Sutton heard the outer door close behind him and then the man behind him spoke again.

"Get his gun, Laureen."

"Gil, I'm afraid of guns. You know I am."

Ellison, Sutton thought.

"Damn you, Laureen!" Ellison exclaimed. "You're more of a hindrance than a help!"

"I got him in here like you told me to do, didn't I?" Laureen snapped as Ellison drew Sutton's .44 from its holster.

"What's going on here, Ellison?" Sutton asked in an even tone.

Ellison's laughter was the only answer he received to his question.

As Ellison's laughter continued and Sutton felt the barrel of the derringer press less firmly against his back, he threw himself to the floor, rolled over, seized one end of the rug covering most of the floor and yanked it toward him.

Ellison let out a roar. His derringer fired, but wildly and the bullet failed even to reach the far end of the stateroom as it blazed above Sutton's head. Ellison, his arms flailing, toppled. Before he hit the floor, Sutton's Colt fell from Ellison's left hand and Sutton made a dive for it. But before he could grasp it, Laureen stepped swiftly forward and kicked it out of his reach.

Sutton reached out and seized her ankles in both hands and pulled on them, sending her sprawling on the floor beside Ellison who was now struggling to rise.

Sutton leaped to his feet and lunged for his Colt which was lying near the dresser. As he was about to bend down to retrieve it, he saw Ellison's reflection in the mirror above the dresser.

As Ellison made a grab for him, Sutton spun around and threw a right jab that caught Ellison squarely on the nose, causing the man to let out another roar. Sutton followed the right jab with a left which connected with Ellison's body just below his ribs.

Ellison's roar died as his breath gusted out of his mouth and he clutched his abdomen with both hands.

Sutton backed up several steps. Without taking his eyes off Ellison who was now doubled over and coughing dryly, he stooped and reached for his Colt.

As he did so, Laureen, who was just out of his line of vision on the far side of the stateroom, seized a crystal vase that was filled with fresh daffodils and hurled it at him.

It struck Sutton a glancing blow on the shoulder and then fell to the floor where it shattered.

Sutton, momentarily off balance, was unprepared for Ellison's sudden move.

As Ellison sprang forward, he delivered a vicious kick that sent a sharp pain stabbing through Sutton's groin. As Ellison drew back his foot a second time, Sutton stiffened, and as his attacker's foot came swinging forward, he seized it, twisted it, and, as Ellison's body was twisted to the left, Sutton let go, rose, and yelled, "Open that door!"

When Laureen, frozen and with her hands covering her mouth, didn't move, he yelled, *"Open it!"*

He seized Ellison from behind by the collar and the seat of the trousers and held him tightly. As Ellison tore fruitlessly at Sutton's fingers which had ripped his celluloid shirt collar, Laureen opened the outer door.

Sutton, holding Ellison several inches off the floor, went through it and out onto the empty deck. A moment later, raising Ellison high above his head as the man screamed wordlessly, he hurled him over the rail and watched as Ellison hit the water and then disappeared beneath its surface.

Sutton turned and raced back into the stateroom—to find Laureen facing him as she stood at the foot of the bed, both of her hands gripping the butt of his Colt which she had retrieved from the floor, her finger on the gun's trigger.

"Looks like you figure now it's your turn to try to do me in," he remarked almost idly but his eyes impaled Laureen where she stood, her lower lip trembling.

"Stay right where you are!" she ordered. "Don't come any closer or I'll shoot. I swear I will. I'll kill you!"

"Now, why would you want to go and do a thing like that?" Sutton took a step toward Laureen, and as he did so her eyes widened and the gun in her hand shook. "And while we're on the subject, why did your friend Ellison try to take me?"

"He told me who you were," Laureen said in a strained voice, "when he left the poker game pretending he wanted a drink. That's when he told me to get you in here. The door behind me, it leads into the Gentlemen's Cabin and, when you and I left there, Gil came in here, unlocked the other door, and then hid behind the deck door to wait for you."

"I'd almost figured all that out for myself," Sutton said. "What I haven't figured out yet though and am not likely to, being a slow-thinking man much of the time, is why you and Gil Ellison took such a nasty interest in me."

"What did you do to Gil? Where his he?"

"I hope he knows how to swim. Or at least dog-paddle."

Laureen stared at Sutton, her brow furrowing, obviously puzzled, but then, as the meaning of what he had said slowly dawned on her, her mouth opened and she gave a wail that rose in intensity and seemed to fill the stateroom with sound.

"He'll *drown!*" she cried a moment later and then took several unsteady steps toward Sutton, fear on her face, her eyes on the open door behind Sutton.

Sutton stepped swiftly forward, seized her wrist with one hand, and with the other tore his .44 from her hand and holstered it.

Laureen, seemingly unaware of what Sutton had done, tried to move around him toward the outer door but he held onto her wrist and spun her around so that she was facing him.

"Now, I want to know what you two were up to and you're going to tell me," he muttered, tightening his grip on Laureen's wrist.

"Don't!" she cried, struggling to free herself but unable to do so.

Sutton heard cries from somewhere outside the stateroom. Then, shouts. He glanced over his shoulder and saw, through the open door that led to the deck, passengers and crewmen running past the stateroom.

"Man overboard!" someone unseen by Sutton shouted.

"Miss Driscoll," he said, "if you have any notions of using that derringer on me—the one over there on the floor that belonged to Ellison—I ought to tell you it's a single-shot weapon and empty at the moment." He released Laureen and ran from the stateroom out onto the deck.

"Throw him a line!"

Sutton looked up to see the captain, who had given the order, standing on the texas deck. He ran to the stern of the boat where a crowd had gathered to the right of the paddle wheel and shouldered his way through it until he could see the barge the boat was towing.

A bedraggled Ellison, his lank brown hair plastered against his forehead, was climbing clumsily up among the lashed-down mining machinery aboard the barge.

"That man!" Ellison screamed once he was safely aboard the barge. He thrust out his arm and pointed directly at Sutton. "That man just tried to kill me!"

Faces turned apprehensively toward Sutton. Both men and women—Jim Collins, Sutton noticed, among them—backed hastily away from him.

"He did!" cried Laureen from behind Sutton. "He tried to kill Mr. Ellison. I was there and I saw him do it. First, he shot at Mr. Ellison and then he threw the poor man overboard!"

"I thought I heard a shot awhile back," murmured a

man in the crowd and the woman standing nervously beside him nodded.

"Seize him!" Ellison shouted, his arm still outstretched, his finger still pointing accusingly at Sutton.

"Wait a minute, folks," Sutton said, holding up his hands as if to keep the uneasy onlookers at bay. "Just let me tell you my side of the story. I—"

But before he could complete what he had been about to say, he felt himself grabbed from behind by two burly crewmen who quickly pinioned his arms behind his back. Someone removed his Colt from its holster.

The captain hurried down the steps from the texas deck and proceeded to give orders to his crew.

When Ellison finally stood dripping on deck in front of Sutton after having been rescued from the barge by a rope thrown to him, he turned to the captain and said, "This man tried to shoot me. Then he threw me into the river."

"Why?" inquired the captain.

"I'll tell you why," Ellison responded. "Laureen, go and get it."

Sutton watched Laureen scurry back along the deck to her stateroom. She reappeared moments later and hurried up to Ellison to whom she handed a folded piece of paper.

"This will provide the answer to your question," Ellison said smugly and handed the paper to the captain who unfolded it and read it.

Ellison said, "I made the mistake of telling him what I knew about him when I learned his name, Captain. He tried to kill me to keep me from telling you—or anyone else—about him."

"Mr. Ellison, you have done all of us a great favor by confronting this criminal so bravely and, at great risk to your own life. But now—well, I'm not quite sure what our next step should be, to speak quite frankly."

"May I be so bold, Captain," Ellison said, "to suggest that you secure Sutton so that he will not pose a threat to anyone else during the remainder of our voyage."

"Yes, yes. I must most certainly do that and will. But then what, Mr. Ellison?"

"I shall be happy to take the murderer off your hands if that's all right with you. I am not averse to collecting the five-hundred-dollar reward offered by the Texas authorities for Sutton's return to their jurisdiction either dead or alive."

"That's a wanted poster you've got there, Captain?" Sutton asked. "With my name on it?"

"It is," the captain replied.

Sutton smiled. "I was a wanted man once. I'm willing to admit that. But I'm not wanted now. You see, what happened was I—"

"Tie him to the deck rail," the captain interrupted, addressing the two crewmen who were still holding Sutton immobile. "Secure him well so that he can cause no more trouble aboard this boat. Be sure to remove that gun belt he's wearing."

"Now, hold on a minute, Captain!" Sutton shouted in exasperation. "You can't do this to me!"

"I can," said the captain flatly and turned away as the two crewmen began to drag Sutton who was still loudly protesting toward the iron rail that circled the deck.

CHAPTER 3

Sutton, his wrists tightly roped to the iron rail, stared up from where he was forced to sit on the deck at Gil Ellison, who was standing and grinning foxily above him.

Both men were silent as the two crewmen who had tied Sutton, satisfied with their handiwork, walked away.

"You gave it a good try, Sutton," Ellison said at last, his grin fading from his face. "But one that just wasn't good enough."

"Maybe I'll get to do a bit better next time," Sutton muttered as the ropes bit into his wrists as if they were bent on shattering his bones.

"There won't be a next time! I'll damn well see to it that there won't be one. You can bank on that, Sutton."

"I had you pegged for a more or less harmless riverboat gambler, Ellison. Didn't so much as guess that you were a bounty hunter too."

"With what I earn gambling and with what Laureen earns—ah, entertaining the men I introduce to her—I do quite well. Bounty hunting is really just a sort of sideline of mine. A way of supplementing my income."

"You're not going to do much supplementing where I'm concerned. Like I told the captain before, I was wanted once in Texas—"

"For the murder of your brother," Ellison interrupted.

"—but I'm not wanted anymore. My name's been cleared."

"It won't work, Sutton, because I don't believe you."

"When this boat stops someplace, you can telegraph the marshal in Virginia City, Nevada. He'll tell you I'm telling the truth."

"I don't have time to sit around in some grimy little river town waiting for word from the sheriff in Virginia City. I'm taking you to Yuma. The sheriff there can contact Texas and, if you are telling the truth, well, all I've lost is a little time and some pride as a result of that dunking you gave me. But if you're lying, and I know very well that you are, you'll sit in a cell and wait until they send someone from Texas to come and collect you and pay me the five hundred dollars due me for apprehending you."

"Some folks believe in always looking on the bright side of things, Ellison. I figure that's what I'd best do at this point. I was heading for Yuma anyway and I won't mind all that much spending a few hours in a jail cell while we wait for word from Texas that it was the truth I told you about me."

Ellison snorted scornfully and strode away across the deck.

Sutton watched him until he disappeared and then was forced to content himself with watching the passengers strolling the deck, some of whom ignored him while others evidently found him intriguing, judging by their wide-eyed stares and wary glances.

He closed his eyes, listening to the grumble of the boilers and the hiss of steam, the slap of water against the boat, the sound of it spilling from the paddle wheel.

He heard light laughter, whispered conversations.

When he opened his eyes again, it was night and he realized that he must have slept. The deck was empty and silent now and he looked up at the red and green passing lights on the stacks high above him.

Time passed and he dozed, awoke, slept again.

He was awake when the boat stopped at Hardyville and the barge was left behind and he remained awake as the boat moved on between tall canyon walls above which he could see a starry slit of dark sky.

Dawn came and died, to be replaced by morning. Later —how much later Sutton couldn't judge for certain because he could not see the sun's position in the sky—a crewman accompanied by Ellison, who held Sutton's .44 in his hand, appeared and proceeded to untie Sutton.

"On your feet," barked the crewman, and when Sutton, his body stiff and most of his muscles cramped because of the awkward position in which he had spent the past uncounted hours, didn't move fast enough to suit him, the crewman reached out, seized Sutton's shoulder, and hauled him roughly to his feet.

"What time is it?" Sutton asked.

"Almost two o'clock. We arrived here at Yuma a little bit behind schedule."

Sutton narrowed his eyes against the sun's glare that glinted off the surface of the river and blazed in reflected brilliance from the extensive scattering of white adobe buildings that were spread out on the river's eastern bank.

When he opened his eyes a moment later, he became aware of the glances that several disembarking men were giving him. He ignored the glances, which were both awed and interested, suggesting that he was some sort of curiosity or, perhaps, freak.

He turned his head and saw the almost completed wooden railroad bridge that stretched from the west bank of the Colorado to within a few yards of the east bank that would soon, he knew, allow the trains of the Southern Pacific Railroad to reach Yuma.

"Let's go, Sutton," Ellison jabbed his prisoner in the back with the barrel of the Colt.

"What about my horse?"

"You've got a horse on board?"

"That bay standing back there by those crates of chickens. He's in need of water and feed."

Ellison beckoned to a crewman, gave an order, and some time later, after Sutton's mount had been watered and fed and then brought to him, he led it down the staging behind Sutton.

Both men were silent as they made their way past the huge Yuma depot into which clattered flatcars piled high with freight unloaded from the *Mojave II* that were being hauled by mules along the track that ran through the center of the depot. When they reached the far end, the braying of mules and the shouts of teamsters filled the air as wagons were loaded with freight before moving out to towns and cities east of Yuma.

They made their way, still silent, through the busy streets and avenues, which bore numbers instead of names, until they reached Main Street and then, a few minutes later, the office of the local sheriff.

Ellison wrapped the reins of Sutton's bay around the hitch rail in front of the office and then ordered Sutton inside.

"What's this?" grumbled the sheriff as Sutton, followed by Ellison, entered the office.

"This," Ellison replied, "is a man wanted for murder." He gave the wanted poster he took from his pocket to the sheriff.

"What the hell am I supposed to do with him?" the sheriff asked, his voice husky as he peered through reddened eyes first at Sutton and then at Ellison.

"Incarcerate him, of course," Ellison answered

smoothly. "And then telegraph to your law enforcement colleagues in Texas to let them know you have him and that they should send someone here to take him back to Texas for trial."

"Mr.—what's your name, bounty hunter?"

"Ellison."

"Well, Mr. Ellison, the fact is I have no room here in the jail for this jasper. We're chock full of disturbers of the peace, horse thieves, and the Lord alone knows how many other kinds of lawbusters. I can't house your prisoner here."

"Sheriff, he's a dangerous man—a murderer. You've got to—"

The sheriff held up a hand and shook a finger in Ellison's face. "Sonny, don't you tell me what I got to do. I'm telling you I got no room in the jail. Now, you caught him. You care for him."

Ellison reached into his pocket. When his left hand emerged from it, a double eagle lay in his palm. He held his hand out to the sheriff.

The sheriff looked down at the coin and then up at Ellison. He reached out and pocketed the money. "You take him up to the territorial prison on the hill outside of town," he told Ellison. "He can cool his heels there till somebody comes to get him. Tell them I sent you."

"Sheriff," Sutton said, "that poster is an old one. It's years old. I'm not a wanted man. Haven't been since about two weeks ago."

"It says here you broke jail," the sheriff commented, squinting at the poster. "You won't break out of our territorial prison, I can guarantee you that."

"Sheriff, you're making a real bad mistake," Sutton declared. "I'm not guilty of anything, and if you'll just telegraph to Texas, they'll tell you so."

"I'll telegraph all right," the sheriff said. "When I get a chance after I've taken care of my far more pressing duties."

"Let's go, Sutton," Ellison said and Sutton again felt the barrel of his own gun bite into his back.

Neither man spoke as they made their way through the town and then began to climb the hill that led to the ominously imposing and fortresslike prison on its summit.

Sutton, as he climbed, looked away from the southern gate of the prison which was a huge arch three times the height of a man into which had been set a lattice of ironwork. The desert stretched out as far as he could see in every direction. The Colorado River was to the north. On his left was the Gila River. To his right was the town of Yuma.

He continued climbing, noting the four guard towers at the corners of the prison whose adobe walls, he estimated, were at least eighteen feet high. Guards were stationed on each of the towers, their faces as grim as the tall walls as they watched Sutton and Ellison approach the gate, rifles in their hands.

"The sheriff sent this prisoner up here," Ellison called out to a guard who was peering quizzically through the ironwork of the arched gate into which a door, also of ironwork, was set.

The guard grumbled words Sutton didn't catch as he unlocked the door and swung it open.

Sutton walked through it and into the large yard where prisoners under guard were excavating cells from solid rock. He quickly surveyed the scene before him. Completed cells, barred by latticed ironwork. A blacksmith's shop. Adobe buildings whose purpose he did not know.

"What's his name and what's he done?" the guard asked

Ellison who replied, "Luke Sutton. Murdered his brother."

The guard's whistle slid shrilly through his yellowed teeth. "We can put him in that cell there. I'll register him as our guest and then put him to work on the rock pile starting tomorrow."

After unlocking the cell door, the guard turned to Sutton and said, "Inside, mister."

Sutton reluctantly entered the cell which measured, he estimated, no more than nine by nine feet and which had a dome of solid rock for a ceiling. On each of two rock walls were bolted three bunks. On every bunk was a dirty straw tick and an equally dirty blanket.

An odorous oak bucket partially filled with urine and feces sat stolidly in the center of the rock floor.

The ironwork door clanged shut behind Sutton and the guard locked it.

Sutton turned and watched the guard and Ellison make their way to a squat adobe building and disappear inside it. He looked up through the lattice and saw the menacing Gatling gun mounted on its two-wheel carriage perched atop the gate tower.

He gripped the lattice and found it absolutely immobile. He turned and examined the rock walls, floor, and ceiling. Obviously impenetrable.

With a shrug, he sat down on the lowest bunk of the tier lining the western wall and bent forward, his forearms resting on his knees, his fingers clasped together.

Bad luck, he thought. That's what it was, no getting around the fact. If Ellison hadn't been a bounty hunter as well as a riverboat gambler . . . If he had taken a boat other than the one Ellison had taken . . .

He wondered how long he would have to spend in this

prison he had once heard a former prisoner refer to—entirely aptly, he thought—as a "hell hole."

As time passed, his thoughts wandered back to that night when one of four men had shot him and another had killed his brother. What had begun that night had ended back in Virginia City, he had believed. But now he knew it had not ended and might never end. Because he had once been a man unjustly wanted for murder and posters had been printed and put in public places offering a five-hundred-dollar reward to the man who brought him in—dead or alive.

He lay back on the bunk, placing his hat over his face and his hands behind his head.

He was up on his feet and reaching for the gun that no longer hung on his hip at the sound of the key turning in the cell door's lock.

Gone, he thought. Ellison's got my gun and my gun belt too. Must have been asleep. How long? He didn't know for sure. But he noticed that the cell was murky and the only sign of sunlight he could detect was a faint glow in the sky above the prison wall in the distance. Sun's setting, he thought, as prisoners filed into the cell and he bent down to retrieve his hat which had fallen to the floor when he had leaped to his feet.

"Who the hell are you?" one of the prisoners asked him.

"A man who finds himself in a peck of trouble," Sutton answered.

His questioner chuckled throatily. "Since you're in Yuma prison, you're in more than a peck of trouble, mister. You're in a bushel of trouble at least."

As the man climbed up onto one of the top bunks, Sutton was about to sit down again on the bunk he had occupied earlier but one of the prisoners, without a word, seized him by the shoulder and shoved him away from it before flopping down upon it himself.

Sutton realized that there were now six men in the cell besides himself which made him realize that he would sleep in no bunk during the coming night.

As a prisoner unbuckled his belt and then proceeded to use the bucket which was the only sanitary facility available inside the cell, Sutton studied the six men who were confined with him. All were dirty and the stench of their unwashed bodies was almost overpowering. All were dull-eyed, slump-shouldered, and wearing clothes that were thick with grime and close, in many cases, to becoming rags.

No, Sutton corrected himself, one's not dull-eyed. That old man watching me's got eyes like lit lamps. Like a cat's eyes come night. Eyes set on fire by fever?

The youngest of the prisoners—Sutton judged him to be no more than fifteen or sixteen—shifted position on his bunk and began to sing softly in Spanish, his song as incongruous to Sutton in the crowded cell as would be the trilling of a meadowlark.

His loose shirt and torn trousers were of white cotton and his brown shoes were scuffed. His black hair was as straight and as long as Sutton's and his skin was the color of honey.

As the boy sang on, his luminous black eyes dreamy, the old man who had been watching Sutton approached him and clutched his sleeve.

"What might be on your mind?" Sutton asked the white-haired and wild-eyed prisoner who began to claw frantically at his arm.

"*Spy!*" the old man hissed, rising and spitting the word into Sutton's ear. "Stay away from him!" The prisoner's hand, more of a claw or a talon, shot out, one finger jabbing in the direction of the boy who had closed his eyes and folded his hands in his lap as he continued singing his faintly doleful song.

"He's a spy, is he?" Sutton asked, glancing at the boy. Then, turning back to the old man who was still clutching his arm, Sutton asked, "Who's he spying on?"

"Me!" the man muttered. His head swung around as he seemed to search the gloomy corners of the cell. "Secret messages," he hissed, reminding Sutton of a snake. "He sends them to the guards. Listen! You hear?"

Sutton recognized a few words and phrases of the boy's song. *Sangre de Cristo. Dios. Padre nuestro.*

"Take it easy, old-timer," Sutton said in a voice meant to be soothing.

"Shut up, dammit!" bellowed one of the other prisoners and the boy's eyes snapped open and his mouth abruptly closed, ending his song.

"You're going to give Parker there another one of his fits!" the same prisoner bellowed, causing the boy to blink nervously.

"Just shut your trap!" the bellowing man flung as a final order at the boy and then turned over on his bunk to face the rock wall.

"They're coming!" screeched the old man, releasing his grip on Sutton's arm. *"They're coming to get me!"*

A howl escaped Parker's lips and in that awful howl Sutton heard both terror and a desperate plea for help.

He put his arm around Parker's shoulder and felt him cringe and then pull away from him. "It's all right. Nobody's coming to get you. The kid was just singing an alabado—a hymn."

Parker's head shook in fearful denial as he glanced at the cell door beyond which now was only darkness and silence. "He sent them a message about me. *Spy!*" As

Parker screamed the last word, he lunged forward, his bony hands reaching for the boy on the bunk who shrank back, his eyes wide with fear mixed with pity.

Sutton seized Parker with both hands and pulled him backward, holding him tightly against his chest as he spoke soothingly to him. "Listen, Parker. I'll straighten things out for you. Now, hold still a minute and *listen!*"

When Parker's struggles ceased momentarily, Sutton winked over the man's shoulder at the boy who had been singing. Then, "Send them a message, kid. Send it now. Tell them to stay away from here, all of them. Tell them to stop bothering my friend Parker here."

The boy again blinked nervously, his uneasy eyes on Sutton.

"Sing that message!" Sutton shouted at him.

The boy's lips parted. A moment later his voice—soft, hushed, almost inaudible—could be heard as he began to sing once again. *"Semana santa . . ."*

When the boy's voice suddenly broke, Sutton winked at him again and said, "That's right. Tell them if they come anywhere near this cell, they'll have me to deal with."

"Padre nuestro . . ."

Sutton released the shuddering Parker. "That ought to do it. You're safe now."

The old man turned toward Sutton, trembling, and looked up into his eyes. "His brothers," he murmured and shot a fearful glance at the cell door. "They said they'd kill me for killing him, and that greaser"—he spun around and pointed an accusing finger at the singing boy—"is one of their spies. If they find me, they'll kill me sure."

"Nobody's going to kill you," Sutton assured Parker. "I'll look out for you. As for that spy over there you're worried about, he won't dare tell anybody where you are. I won't let him."

"He deserved killing, Mal Folsom did," the old man told Sutton in an almost steady voice, his head bobbing to reinforce his words. "Stole my woman, Mal Folsom did, just last week. So I killed him. I've been on the run from those brothers of his since."

"Well, you can stop running now," Sutton assured the man. "Nobody'll find you here. You're safe here from the Folsoms."

Parker took a step away from Sutton, his eyes narrowing. Then, another step. A third. "You're Folsom," he said, his voice a sigh. "You're Mal Folsom in the flesh! That spy —he sent you word where I was." Parker continued moving backward and, when Sutton took a step toward him, Parker shrieked, his back pressed against the far wall of the cell.

His shrieking continued, splitting the night's silence, and nothing Sutton could do could quiet the man.

"Guard!" yelled one of the prisoners. And again, at the top of his voice, *"Guard!"*

A guard arrived a moment later, took one look into the cell, called for assistance, and, moments later, three guards dragged Parker, still shrieking, from the cell, his body shuddering and his eyes rolling in his head.

"I warned you, Arista," snapped the prisoner who had earlier shouted at the boy who had been singing. "I told you your caterwauling'd give Parker another one of his fits."

"It wasn't the boy's fault," Sutton said. "It's plain to see that Parker's loco."

"Sure, he's loco," the prisoner agreed. "But he stays quiet less'n that Arista starts in to baying at the moon like he just went and done. Now none of us is going to get a good night's sleep. Arista, I've a good mind to come over there and gouge out both of your eyeballs and stomp on them till they're mush."

Sutton stepped in front of the prisoner as he started to rise from his bunk. He said nothing. He merely stood, his fists clenched at his sides, staring down at the prisoner on the bunk.

"Aw, t' hell with Arista," the man barked. "T' hell with you too, whoever you are."

As the man turned over on his bunk to face the rock wall, Sutton crossed the cell. He was about to sit down on the floor when Arista said, "I thank you, señor. I did not mean to cause trouble. But I sing the alabados because they lift a heavy load from my heart. I meant no harm."

"It's not your fault what happened," Sutton said as the sound of the still-shrieking Parker, distant now, drifted into the cell.

Sutton held out his hand. "Name's Luke Sutton."

"Paco Arista," the boy said and shook Sutton's hand.

"Where'd they take Parker?"

"To the crazy hole."

"The crazy hole? What's that?"

Arista shifted position on his bunk and gestured. When Sutton had seated himself beside Arista, the boy answered, "The hole is a small cell. It is made of hollowed-out rock like the others—like this one. Many prisoners go crazy here. The heat. The life—how it is lived here. The years—so slow they go by. When a man goes crazy and causes trouble—he goes to the hole until he is quiet once more."

"Parker said he killed a man last week. He don't look strong enough to kill a man, feeble as he is. Or to have a woman either, for that matter."

"Ah, it is his mind. The dreams he dreams there. They say the old one did kill a man who tried to take his woman.

A man named Mal Folsom. But that, they say, happened ten—some say twenty—years ago. He was in prison for life in Prescott. But when they built this place they sent him here. To dream his dreams. To die his death."

"You been here long?" Sutton asked Arista.

"Seven months. Like the old one, I too killed a man." Sutton remained silent.

"My sister, she is thirteen. Vaqueros came to our village of Rosario. To our cantina. They saw my sister in the plaza. When night came, they took her. I heard her scream. I ran to find her and when I did, I pulled the man off her and shot him through the head with my father's pistol. Now I am here."

"They oughtn't to put boys in a place like this," Sutton remarked.

Arista's eyes blazed. "I am sixteen. I am a man."

"Sorry, Paco. I shouldn't've said what I did. Any fellow who fights to save his sister's honor like you did, well, there's no doubt he's a man."

"You will be here long, Luke?"

Sutton knew what Arista was really asking, so he answered, "They've got me here because they think I'm wanted for murder in Texas. They're wrong. I'm not. I ought to be out of here by tomorrow or the next day at the latest."

Arista sighed softly. "I wish, truly, that I could say the same. Soon it will be *semana santa*—Holy Week. In my village of Rosario, it is a good time. We Penitentes—for us it is a more important time than Christmas."

"I've heard tales told about the Penitentes. It's true that you fellows whip yourselves bloody of your own free will?"

Arista nodded. "We use the *disciplinas* on ourselves, yes, it is so."

"Disciplinas?"

"Whips we make of cactus roots."

"Now, don't get me wrong, Paco. I don't mean to be insulting but I'd like to understand why you do like you do."

Again Arista nodded, his eyes appraising Sutton, as he said, with pride evident in his voice, "We believe we must suffer—must make ourselves suffer for our sins so that then we may be free of them. We are Los Penitentes de la Sangre de Cristo."

"The penitents of the blood of Christ," Sutton translated.

"Ah, you speak Spanish."

"No, Paco, I don't. But I've picked up a few words of your lingo along some of the trails I've traveled. Enough for me to understand some of what I hear spoken in Spanish but I'm in no way smart or clever enough to speak sensible Spanish."

"I wish to be there in Rosario for *semana santa,*" Arista murmured and added wistfully, "but I shall not be there."

Sutton was silent as Arista began to sing again in an almost inaudible voice.

"Sangre de Cristo . . ."

The holy words of Arista's hymn blended with the demented ones of Parker that Sutton heard still being shouted in the dark distance.

As Arista continued to sing softly of the spilled blood of Christ, Parker loudly told the heedless night about the spies that were everywhere and after him.

CHAPTER 4

The loud grating of a rifle barrel being drawn along his cell's lattice of ironwork shattered Sutton's sleep just after dawn the following morning.

As the guard outside the cell yelled, "On your feet animals, and let's get moving!" Sutton rose from Parker's bunk where he had spent the night.

The guard swung the cell door open and Sutton moved out with the other prisoners to join those already gathered in the large courtyard.

He marched with them to the dining room and sat down on a bench next to Arista. He reached out for the huge bowl that sat in the center of the table but a prisoner opposite him struck his wrist with a clenched fist and seized the bowl.

Sutton half rose, reached out, and tipped the bowl so that the cornmeal mush it contained spilled on the shirt and trousers of the man who had struck him. "You ought to learn to mind your manners," he told the man. "I've heard of boardinghouse reach but not boardinghouse assault and battery."

"Be quiet," Arista whispered to him.

"You saw what he did," Sutton responded. "Nearly busted my wrist. Pass me that basket of bread, Paco."

Sutton saw the alarmed look on Arista's face but before he could ask what had caused it, he was seized from behind by a guard and hauled to his feet.

Sutton broke free of the man's grip, spun around, and sent a fist slamming into the guard's jaw which unbalanced him and caused him to fall against the prisoners seated at the table behind him.

"Luke, don't!" Arista pleaded, his words loud in the dining room's sudden silence.

Guards came running from every direction, rifles in their hands, and surrounded Sutton as the guard he had punched got to his feet and threw a fist that landed below Sutton's belt, doubling him over and causing him to gasp for breath.

"No talking's allowed while you're in here," the guard said to him, smirking. "That's the rule and you'd better remember it."

"Nobody had the good grace to tell me about your rule," Sutton muttered as he straightened up and his breathing slowed.

"Fighting with other prisoners ain't allowed either," the guard added as if Sutton had not spoken.

"You got your rules and regulations," Sutton said, his voice low, "but I've got my rights and one of them's I don't belong here in the first place. In the second place, I don't take too kindly to the kind of treatment you hand out when you've got a bunch of other guards with guns aimed right at me. That's a cowardly way to try to take a man."

"You calling me a coward?" The guard glared menacingly at Sutton.

"I am. Now, I want to see the man in charge of this prison and I want to see him right now. I plan on telling him a thing or two, one of which is that he oughtn't to hire bullies like you."

"I may be a coward and I may be a bully," the guard told Sutton with a gloating smile on his face, "but there's one other thing I am and that's your keeper while you're in here. While you're in here your soul may belong to God Almighty but your body's mine. You understand that?"

Sutton swung and his left jab connected with the side of the guard's head.

As the guard threw a right uppercut, Arista leaped to his feet and grabbed Sutton by the shoulder. "Sit down, Luke. Please, Luke, sit—"

The guard swung a beefy arm and sent Arista sprawling on the floor.

Sutton, enraged, was about to go for the guard again when he was knocked to his knees by the butt of a rifle that landed at the base of his skull. On all fours on the floor, he shook his head groggily as little white lights flickered in front of his eyes.

"What's going on here?" asked someone whose voice seemed to Sutton to be coming from a great distance.

He heard other voices then but not all the words that were spoken. He reached out, got a grip on a bench, and managed to struggle to his feet.

"You're the prisoner who was brought in yesterday," declared the man who was standing warily a safe distance away from Sutton.

"That's Sutton, Superintendent," said one of the guards. "He was talking and he tried to incite a riot."

"You the one in charge of this outhouse?" Sutton asked the gaunt man facing him.

"I am Superintendent Thurlow, yes."

"Well, I got something to say to you, Thurlow." Sutton hurriedly explained about Ellison and the wanted poster and then about having asked the sheriff in Yuma to telegraph the Texas authorities to confirm his claim that he was not a wanted man.

Arista, on his feet now, turned to Thurlow and said,

"Señor, it was not Luke's fault. A prisoner hit him and he—"

"A prison can operate properly," intoned Thurlow, "only if discipline is maintained. You, Sutton, show signs of incorrigibility which, if not curbed and curbed firmly at the outset will eat like acid at the orderliness that is the basis of a well-run penal institution such as this one. You and your fellow troublemaker—"

"Paco's no troublemaker. He tried to keep me from hitting your guard again. He—"

Before turning away, Thurlow said, "Take them both to the disciplinary dungeon. They will remain there for five days."

"Señor, not the snake den!" Arista cried. "We will make no more trouble if—"

Thurlow looked haughtily down at the cringing Arista and remarked, "You are quite correct, Paco. Neither of you will make any more trouble after you have both spent five days in the disciplinary dungeon. However, if either of you do make trouble in the future after you have served your time in the dungeon, you will be returned there for *ten* days."

"Wait a minute!" Sutton shouted as the guards began to drag him and Arista from the dining room. "I told you I'm not guilty of anything!" he shouted to Thurlow's retreating back. "And what's more, Paco didn't do nothing but try to—"

"Shut up!" snarled one of the guards as Sutton and Arista were dragged out into the courtyard.

Shackles were brought and placed on both men's ankles and wrists before they were prodded by four guards down a narrow passageway and into a rock-walled cell that was almost completely dark.

As the dungeon's door was closed and locked, Sutton

stared through its iron slats into the sunlight at the far end of the passageway.

Arista groaned and bumped into him.

"What's wrong, Paco?"

Arista was squinting at the floor, his head moving from side to side. "Snakes come here sometimes. Sidewinders. That is why we call this place the snake den."

Sutton moved about the cell that measured, he estimated, about ten by ten feet, his shackles rattling, his eyes on the rock floor, keenly aware of the stench that pervaded the poorly ventilated cell. He found no snakes.

"There's not so much as a bucket for a man to use in here," he observed grimly.

Arista said nothing as he sat down near the cell door and wrapped his arms around his bent knees.

"I'm sorry to've got you mixed up in my trouble, Paco. If I'd've known you were going to step in, I'd've kept a tighter rein on my temper."

Arista shrugged. "It is nothing. A thing one does for a friend."

"It's not nothing, Paco. It's something, is what it is, and I want you to know I appreciate it." Sutton sat down with his back against the far wall to wait for time to pass, to wait for five days to come and go.

At times, he slept. When awake, he paced the cell, stretched his body, exercised to rid his muscles of stiffness.

An unknown amount of time later, a guard came down the passageway, opened the cell door, and placed a pitcher and two pieces of bread just inside the door. Then he dropped a snuffbox he had taken from his pocket, causing its lid to snap open, he cursed and then retrieved the box.

When he had gone, Sutton picked up the pitcher and

drank some of the water before offering it to Arista who
shook his head.

Sutton picked up one of the pieces of bread and held it
out to Arista who again shook his head.

"Hey, Paco, it's not much I'll admit but it is something.
It'll at least keep us alive till we get out of here."

"I have told you, Luke, how it is in here—the life—and
you have seen it for yourself. I do not want to live in this
way so I have decided to die."

"You can stick it out, Paco. It may not be all that easy but
you can learn to grin and bear it, and once you get out
again—"

"I will never again get to live outside these walls."

"You mean to say you drew a life sentence for shooting
that rapist?"

It was Arista's turn to nod.

Sutton sat down beside the boy. "A man's no good to
himself or anybody else once he's dead. Alive, though, he
might find a way to make things better for himself. Paco,
you told me you were a man and I know that to be true.
Now, a man don't just decide to die. He fights for his life."

"How? In here how may a man fight for his life?"

Sutton met Arista's questioning gaze. He placed one of
the two pieces of bread in the boy's hand. "By eating this
bread for starters. I don't have so many friends that I can
afford to lose even one of them."

Arista accepted the bread and then hungrily devoured
it.

Sutton gave him the pitcher of water and watched him
drink.

Arista suddenly let out a cry and sprang to his feet,
dropping the pitcher.

"What's wrong, Paco?"

"Scorpion!" Arista cried and pointed to his leg.

Sutton saw the venomous creature, its tail curved up and over its back, crawling up the leg of Arista's trousers. Sutton raised one leg and, hopping about on the other, pulled off his boot and used it to knock the scorpion to the floor. He crushed it under his other boot and then glanced at the trembling Arista.

"I thought you'd decided to die. That scorpion could have helped you on your way with one flick of its tail."

Arista turned sharply to face Sutton, saw his grin, and then grinned faintly himself. "The guard," he said. "He brought it. In that snuffbox he dropped."

"They do things like that to prisoners here?"

"That is what the men here say."

"Then you and me we'd best be about keeping our eyes wide open from now on until we're let out of here."

Day was ending when a guard unlocked the dungeon door on the fifth day after Sutton and Arista had been imprisoned.

He gestured peremptorily and both men, their shackles clanking as they walked down the narrow passageway, emerged blinking into the last rays of the day's setting sun.

"I want to see Superintendent Thurlow," Sutton told the guard.

The guard merely gestured to summon another guard who set about removing the shackles from Sutton's and Arista's wrists and ankles.

"I got to find out if the sheriff in town's had word about me from Texas," Sutton persisted.

"You don't need to see Thurlow for that," the first guard remarked. "I can tell you what you're so anxious to find out."

Sutton waited a moment and then, when the guard said no more, snapped, "Tell me!"

"Looks like you'll be staying with us awhile longer, Sutton. Our sheriff, he got word about you—from a Sheriff Britton in Texas. Britton telegraphed that he'd sent a man up to Virginia City where he'd been told you were a week or so ago and it seems he was real surprised to find out you were down here in Yuma Prison. Anyway, the long and the short of it is, he wants you kept here till the deputy he's sending to get you arrives and pays off the bounty hunter who caught you."

"But that makes no kind of sense!" Sutton protested.

"It's time to move out," the guard announced when the shackles had been removed and the guard who had removed them had gone. "To the dining room. Quick march!"

Once inside the dining room, Sutton sat down next to Arista and both men greedily devoured the first decent meal they had had since entering the dungeon. For five days a daily ration of bread and water had been their only sustenance.

Neither man spoke. The only sounds in the room were those of men eating and the *tinging* of tin utensils against tin plates.

The guards stood with their backs to the room's walls, their eyes roving over the prisoners, their hands on their rifles.

Superintendent Thurlow came through the dining-room door and strode up to a raised dais at the far end of the room. As he turned toward the prisoners, the sounds of turning wagon wheels and jingling harness drifted into the room from the courtyard beyond it.

"Men, I have good news for you," Thurlow announced. "Some ladies from town—members of the renowned

Yuma Glee Club—have just arrived to present a program appropriate to Easter which we will all gratefully and reverently observe on Sunday next. I am quite certain you will find the music uplifting and I expect you all to remain silent as a way of showing proper respect for the ladies who have come here with your best interests at heart."

Thurlow beckoned and a group of women entered and made their way between the tables toward the dais, their eyes on Thurlow as if they dared not look a single prisoner in the face.

"Switch places with me," Sutton whispered to Arista. *"Sshhh!"*

Sutton ignored Arista's sibilant warning and, as the guards' eyes followed the women who were mounting the dais, he quickly rose and shoved Arista into his former position on the bench before sitting down at the end of the bench where Arista had been sitting.

"Sutton!"

Sutton gave the guard who had spoken his name an innocent glance.

"If you're fixing to start more trouble," the guard muttered, "you'll land right back where you just came from."

"Haven't seen so many pretty females in one place since the last church picnic I went to," Sutton told the guard. "Just wanted to get me the best look possible at each and every one of them, so I switched seats."

"Shut up, Sutton!"

Sutton shrugged and, ignoring the guard, turned his attention to the women on the dais.

"Ready, ladies?" inquired a matronly woman who now faced the cluster of nine women with her back to her audience of prisoners. She raised both arms expectantly and then began to wave them wildly about as the choristers burst into shrill song.

Sutton listened to the soprano rendering of a hymn he had never heard before, his mind racing, the guard beside him visible out of the corner of his eye.

"*. . . wending their sorrowful way to the tomb . . .*"

He began to hum along with the enthusiastically singing women, causing the guard to nudge him in the ribs with the barrel of his rifle.

"*. . . and, lo, the stone was rolled back . . .*"

Sutton, silent now, eased to his right.

"*Hallelujah!*" chorused the women. "*Sinners, rejoice in your redemption!*"

Sutton suddenly sprang to his feet and swiftly wrested the rifle from the surprised guard's hands.

"*Hallelujah!*" repeated the singers, eyes gazing heavenward.

"Arista!" Sutton said. "On your feet and let's get the hell out of here!"

"*Heaven is our heritage . . .*"

"Damn you, Sutton!" shouted the guard, making a grab for the rifle Sutton had taken from him.

Sutton clubbed the guard on the side of his head with the rifle butt.

Arista, his eyes wide and his mouth open in amazement, leaped up from the bench.

One of the singers screamed. The singing and the guard collapsed.

Women's screams began to fill the dining room as an armed guard raced toward Sutton through the rows of tables.

Sutton fired the rifle in his hands, putting a bullet into the floor just in front of the man's feet.

The guard abruptly halted.

"Seize him!" Thurlow screamed, pointing at Sutton, his gaunt face flushed.

"Anybody makes a move," Sutton yelled, hoping he could be heard above the frightened shrieks of the women on the dais, "guard or prisoner, and he's as good as dead." He began to back toward the dining-room door. "Arista, drag that guard outside. The three of us are about to take a trip together."

One of the guards suddenly fired at Sutton but his shot missed, embedding itself in the wall to Sutton's left.

Sutton got off a snap shot which went over the heads of both the guard and the women directly behind him.

A woman swooned, falling into the trembling arms of one of her companions.

"Thurlow, tell your boys not to try to take me," Sutton shouted. "They do, they're dead. I missed your man on purpose. But next time, I'll kill on purpose. Maybe you. Maybe one of your lady rejoicers up there on the dais. Now, tell me, Thurlow. Would you want a thing like that to happen?"

Sutton's words caused two more women to swoon. Moments later, the dais was littered with limp bodies.

Sutton, at the dining-room door, waited until Arista had dragged the unconscious guard through it and then he himself backed out. "Get the guard into that wagon," he ordered Arista who hastily obeyed him.

After leaping up onto the seat, Sutton handed the rifle to Arista, grabbed the reins of the team that was hitched to the wagon, and yelled up to the two guards who were climbing the gate tower to the prison's Gatling gun. "We got one of your boys in the wagon here! You shoot and we kill him. Now, open the gate!"

Sutton clucked to the team, turned them, and headed for the gate past the hivelike cells on one side and the adobe administration buildings on the other.

"Luke!" Arista shouted. "The gate it is not opening. We will hit it!"

Sutton's only response was to urge the team into a gallop.

He was almost at the gate before the guard posted beside it managed to unlock and swing it wide open.

"Hallelujah!" Sutton roared happily at the top of his voice as he drove the wagon through the gate and then down the hill, heading for the desert.

"Santa Maria!" exclaimed Arista who was crouching and crossing himself in the wagon bed behind Sutton.

Sutton slapped the rumps of the team with the leather reins and the wagon continued careening down the hill toward the Gila River in the distance. "Where's your village, Paco?" he yelled over his shoulder.

"Rosario," Arista yelled back as the wagon racketed along, "it is east of here and about fifteen miles south of the river."

Sutton turned the team and headed east, paralleling the river's course.

"We are going to Rosario?" Arista called out, excitement giving an edge to his voice.

"You got some place better to go?"

"No!"

"Then Rosario, here we come!"

They had not gone more than a few hundred yards when Sutton heard Arista let out an alarmed yell. He looked back over his shoulder to find the guard on his feet, his rifle once again in his hands and aimed now at Sutton's back.

"Stop the wagon!" the guard yelled. *"Now!"*

Sutton hesitated but then, as he saw the guard's finger tighten on the trigger, he reined in the team.

A moment after the horses came to a halt, he suddenly

slapped them with the reins and they bolted forward, unbalancing the guard who fell over the side of the wagon to the ground, his rifle accidentally discharging as he did so.

Sutton soon had the horses galloping again. He yelled to Arista to get down in the wagon bed as the sound of a rifle shot came from behind them.

Sutton hunkered down as low as he could with his body tilted to the right and pressed against the back of the wagon seat for protection.

A second shot tore past him as the team galloped on. Minutes later, he straightened up again since he was certain they were out of range of the guard's gun by now.

"You okay back there?" he called out to Arista.

"*Sí.* But I still do not believe it."

"Believe what?"

"Everything," Arista said as he climbed over the wagon seat and seated himself beside Sutton in the deepening darkness. "It all happened so fast. Like lightning."

"I can move fast when I've a mind to."

"Like lightning," Arista repeated and Sutton gave him a grin. "Luke, it was a lie you told me?"

"I never lied to you."

"But you said you were innocent. The guard said the sheriff telegraphed from Texas to say that you are a wanted man—"

"It took me some time to figure out why Sheriff Britton was sending a deputy to Yuma to fetch me but then it all came clear. Back in Virginia City the marshal was after me on account of he thought I'd killed my brother down in Texas. He got his hands on me and sent word to Texas—to the sheriff there—to send a deputy to pick me up. But then the marshal found out I wasn't guilty.

"The deputy sent to Virginia City from Texas to get me

hadn't arrived by the time I'd left town. Maybe he never did arrive for one reason or another. Anyway, when the sheriff in Yuma telegraphed to Texas about me, the sheriff there had no way of knowing at that time that I'd already cleared my name of the killing of my brother before I ever left Virginia City."

"Ah," Paco sighed. "I did not think you would lie to a friend."

"About how far's your village from Yuma, Paco?"

"Sixty miles."

"We ought to get there sometime tomorrow."

"I will be happy to be back home in Rosario again. I will be happy to see my father and sister again. They will be glad that I come home for *semana santa*." Arista smiled dreamily. "Luke, tell the horses to hurry."

"You heard him," Sutton said, addressing the team. *"Gee up!"*

They arrived in Rosario early the following morning to find the small village eerily silent and seemingly empty.

"Where's everybody?" Sutton asked as he halted the team and jumped down from the wagon.

Arista climbed down to stand beside him. "They make ready for the Good Friday service. It will be held there— in the morada."

Sutton looked in the direction Arista was pointing and saw the windowless adobe building in front of which stood a huge cross made of hand-adzed logs.

"The *calvario*," Arista declared, pointing to the cross. "Come. We go now to my father's house."

Sutton followed Arista to a small adobe dwelling some distance from the morada. He stood beside the door as Arista's father and sister cried out in surprise at the sight of their son and brother before running to him and embracing him. Tears flowed. Hands touched tenderly. Kisses were exchanged. Spanish words tumbled over one another, occasionally drowning in happy laughter.

Arista at last disengaged himself from the arms of his ebony-eyed sister and pointed to Sutton. He spoke rapidly in Spanish, his eyes glowing brightly in the light of the lantern that sat on a wooden table in the center of the room.

His father spoke in Spanish and then Arista spoke again as his sister shot shy glances in Sutton's direction.

"I don't want to ruin your homecoming, Paco," Sutton said. "If someone in your village will sell me a horse and saddle—and some kind of sidearm—I'll be on my way."

Arista spoke to his father who nodded and then to his sister who fled from the room. "You will stay here with us for a little time," Arista said.

Sutton wasn't sure if he had been given an order or asked a question.

Arista's father came up to Sutton, embraced him, kissed him on both cheeks, and spoke rapidly in Spanish.

"He says," Arista translated, "that you are welcome to his house and to all he owns for saving his beloved son."

"Tell your pa I appreciate his sentiments, Paco, but tell him that you were the one who saved your own skin."

Arista smiled as his father stepped back from Sutton and his sister flew back into the room, speaking so fast Sutton couldn't recognize a single word of her Spanish.

Arista said, "She says a horse and saddle are being brought here to the house. The best in the village. And a gun too. But I say to you, Luke, do not go. Stay here with us. Rest. Eat."

"Well, I've got something to do that needs doing real bad, Paco, and I've been kept from doing it too long as it is, but—"

Sutton didn't finish his sentence. Instead, he turned around to peer through the open door as the sound of singing reached his ears.

"It begins," Arista told him. "The women, they come and bring the *Madre Dolorosa.*"

Sutton watched the procession of women wend their way through the village, singing mournfully and bearing on their shoulders a plank platform on which knelt a young woman robed and veiled in blue with her hands clasped in front of her—the Mother of Sorrows.

"Luke, look." Arista pointed in the opposite direction.

Sutton saw a second procession, this one composed of men, wending their way toward the morada from the opposite direction bearing another plank platform on which stood, in a posture of abject humility, a man whose entire body was hidden from view by the purple robe he was wearing. On his bowed head rested a crown of thorns and a black blindfold covered his eyes.

"The Son," Arista whispered in an awed tone.

Suddenly, some of the Penitentes following the man portraying the Christ figure began to blow on the pipes they carried, creating mournful music. Others among them stripped off their shirts and, using the whips they called *disciplinas* or lengths of chain, began to flagellate their bare backs. At the same time, the women broke into a loud wailing.

Matracas in the hands of some of the Penitentes began to whir ominously, filling the air with a portent of doom. Clackers in the hands of others snapped and snarled in the hot air.

"Mother and Son will soon meet," Arista said. "Then they will go into the morada where the darkness of death will soon descend."

Sutton suddenly turned his attention from the two

processions because he thought he had heard a sound that was not made by *matracas,* clackers, or pipes. The sound of hoofbeats.

When he saw the five riders heading across the desert toward the village, his eyes narrowed and he held his hand over them to shield them from the glare of the sun as he watched the men approach.

"A posse!" he muttered to Arista. "Of prison guards. They're after us, Paco!"

"We must hide, Luke."

"Where?"

"Here—here in the house."

"No good. They'll search every inch of every house in the village. Turn them all upside down looking for us." Sutton's gaze swept the village, coming to rest on the Mother and Son as the two processions met and melded together. He seized Arista by the arm. "What did you mean before—about the darkness of death in the morada?"

"The candles—they are put out to mean that the Son is dead."

"Paco, listen up. Here's what we're going to do." Sutton quickly outlined the plan he had only that instant formulated as the Penitentes gathered under the shadow of the huge cross outside the morada. "You tell them what they've got to do!"

Sutton seized Paco's arm and they went running toward the crowd who were placing the platforms on the ground.

When they reached the Penitentes, Arista spoke rapidly in Spanish and, even before he had finished, the man portraying the Christ began to remove his robe, blindfold, and crown of thorns.

As Sutton bent down and scooped up dirt to rub on his

face and hands to darken his complexion, the woman representing Mary slipped out of her blue robe and veil and handed them to Arista who quickly donned them.

Sutton tossed his hat to the ground and took the purple robe from the man who had been wearing it and who now was holding it out to him. Sutton wrapped it around his body as the crowd formed a protective circle around him and Arista. He winced as he placed the sharp crown of thorns on his head and then tied the black blindfold around his eyes. It covered half of his forehead and part of his nose, but by looking straight down, he could see the ground for a short distance in front of him.

One of the men in the crowd stepped up to the heavy wooden door of the morada and knocked on it three times.

Sutton heard the bar behind it being raised and then the sound of it opening.

Arista took him by the arm, ready to lead him into the morada, but he froze as the five prison guards rode up and drew rein, dust billowing out behind them.

"Halt!" yelled their leader.

The crowd halted but no one turned around.

"We've got reason to believe that two prisoners who escaped from the territorial prison are here in this village. Are they?"

An old man turned to face the leader of the posse. "Señor, this it is a holy day. We hold religious services to mark the death of Christ. Go away and leave us in peace."

The man gestured and the other four riders dismounted, each of them entering one of the houses that bordered the village's single street. As the other people in the crowd turned toward him, he scanned their faces intently.

As the posse fanned out to search the village, Sutton felt

Arista's hand grip his arm and, followed by the Penitentes, he let himself be led into the morada.

Matracas began to whir. Pipes sounded. Thirteen candles, seven on one side of an altar and six on the other, blazed. A man stepped up to the altar and began to sing in Spanish and the people behind him, kneeling now, gave him their soft responses.

"You said it was going to be dark in here," Sutton said to Arista who stood by his side.

"It will be," Arista assured him.

The singing continued and during it Sutton and Arista took up positions to one side of the only door leading into the morada.

Some time later, the door was thrown open and the five members of the posse burst into the midst of the assembled crowd.

"Where are they?" one of the men thundered.

No one answered him as the man who was leading the singing stepped up to the altar and began to extinguish the candles one by one until only a single candle remained burning.

"We're getting out of here," Sutton whispered to Arista. "Tell your people to bar the door as soon as we're gone to keep these jaspers locked up in here for as long as they can."

Arista whispered in Spanish to a man next to him and the man nodded eagerly.

"Stop!" the leader of the posse shouted at the man standing in front of the altar who was about to extinguish the remaining candle.

But the man did not stop. Instead, he reached out and extinguished the final candle, plunging the interior of the morada into total darkness.

Sutton tore the blindfold from his eyes, grabbed Arista

with one hand, and with the other opened the door and went outside, shutting it behind him.

Inside the morada, men and women began to shriek and wail. Chains rattled. Pipes shrilled.

As Sutton and Arista ran, pausing only long enough for Sutton to retrieve his hat, the bedlam inside the morada increased in intensity.

Screams shredded the air as the Penitentes mourned the death of their Savior.

Sutton, still running, threw away his crown of thorns and shrugged out of his purple robe. Arista ran beside him, doffing his robe and veil as he did so.

"Behind my father's house!" Arista called out to Sutton. "The horse."

When Sutton ran around behind the Arista's house he found a saddled and bridled dun. He looked back over his shoulder. "Paco! Where are you?"

Arista appeared a moment later and sprinted up to Sutton. "Here is the gun you wanted. I found it inside the house."

Sutton took the blunt-barreled sheriff's model Colt and thrust it into his waistband. "I hope your people barred the morada door," he muttered as he quickly climbed into the saddle.

"I told them to do so."

"Up you go, Paco."

When Arista was seated behind him on the dun, Sutton dug his heels into the animal's flanks and the horse went galloping away from Rosario toward the desert.

CHAPTER 5

Sutton and Arista had been riding for less than an hour when Arista tapped Sutton on the shoulder and said, "Stop, Luke."

"Stop? And maybe let that posse trim our tails for us?"

"Please, Luke."

Sutton drew rein and Arista slid down over the rump of the dun.

"This is as far as I go, Luke."

Sutton studied his companion's face a moment before stating, "You look like a man whose mind's set on something."

"*Sí.* I will go into those mountains there." Arista pointed at the small range to the south. "I will stay there for a while and then go back to Rosario. The guards will be gone. I will take my father and my sister and we will go away. To a place where we will not be found."

"Superintendent Thurlow might have a man—or men —stationed at your village figuring you'll come back."

"It might be so," Arista agreed solemnly. And then, smiling, he said, "I will be clever like the cougar. I will watch. Wait. Only when I am sure it is safe will I return. And then only to go quickly away again to a safe place with my family."

"Well, Paco, I wish you the best of luck."

"Luke, where do you go?"

Sutton glanced to the east. "I'm heading for a town

called Dead Horse that's supposed to be situated somewhere along the Gila River though I don't know where
exactly. But I expect if I just keep going, I'll stumble on it
sooner or later." He thrust a hand into his boot, pulled out
his money, and counted out fifty dollars. He gave them to
Arista and returned the rest to his boot.

Arista, startled, tried to return the money but Sutton
shook his head.

"Paco, that there cash is to pay for this horse and his
gear that I've got under me, thanks to the kindness of your
pa." He withdrew the Colt from his waistband and
handed it to Arista. "You might have need of this."

"But without it you—"

"I'll manage. I'll be fine."

"No," Arista said, shaking his head. "This is wrong. The
horse—the gun—they were gifts given to thank you for
helping me escape from prison."

"I told you once and I'll tell you again. You saved your
own skin. Now the trick's for you to keep it all in one
piece."

Sutton bent down and shook hands with Arista. *"Adiós,*
Paco."

"Adiós, Luke."

Sutton rode away feeling decidedly uncomfortable
without the Colt but he did not regret his decision to give
it to the boy. He had not gone far when he glanced back
over his shoulder to find Arista standing and watching
him. He raised his arm and waved. When Arista returned
his wave, he rode on and this time he didn't look back.

For the next three days, traveling mainly by night and
taking whatever shelter he could find during the day, he
followed the river, turning north on the second day at
Gila Bend, then east, and then southeast on the third day.
The eastern stretch of the Lower Colorado Valley through

which he rode was a vast stretch of hot and apparently lifeless desert broken only occasionally by widely scattered mountain ranges.

Sutton passed occasional stands of mesquite and the desert was dotted in places with creosote bush and white bur sage. On the fourth day of his journey, his keen eyes, ever watchful, spotted the widely spaced tracks of a bannertail kangaroo rat which had hopped along at right angles to his path. He turned the dun and followed the tracks—some separated by as much as five feet—until he reached the animal's communal burrow.

He dismounted and tore a piece of cloth from the tail of his shirt to rig a looped fish snare, not to catch a bannertail, but the bannertail's natural predator. He took up a position behind a nearby giant saguaro cactus to wait. His wait was rewarded when the sun was almost down and he spotted the kit fox following the scent left by the kangaroo rat. When the fox reached the rat's burrow, which had been plugged to seal out the heat of the day, Sutton's fingers tightened on the end of his snare line. Then, as the fox padded cautiously forward on its hairy paws, which gave it traction in the soft sand, and began to claw at the debris blocking the entrance to the burrow, Sutton jerked the line. His prey thrashed violently about on the ground in its frantic efforts to free itself.

Sutton rose and dragged the animal toward him. He seized it by the scruff of its neck to avoid being bitten and smashed the animal's skull against the side of a rocky formation that sprouted next to him. After skinning the animal with a sharp stone in a crude fashion and gutting it with his fingers, he ate the bloody carcass raw before resuming his journey.

It was early the following morning when he came to a

small settlement, a cluster of less than half a dozen adobe buildings.

A man lounged idly against one of the buildings, watching Sutton approach.

"Morning," Sutton greeted him. "Might this be the town of Dead Horse?"

The man shook his head, spat a stream of tobacco juice, wiped his lips with the back of his hand, and remarked, "It's Dead Horse you're after?"

"That's right. I am."

"Dead Horse," the man repeated. "That place is a regular metropolis compared to this place here. This place isn't much more than a place to squat for men like me. We'll probably die both broke and crazy looking for gold or maybe silver around here."

"You fellows find any?"

"Some. Not much. Not near enough to keep body and soul together. We find copper from time to time. But it costs more than the ore's worth to pack it to Yuma so's it can be sent for smelting to Wales—place called Swansea across the pond."

"How far's it to Dead Horse?"

The man seemed to ponder the question. "You mean in miles or hours?"

"Either way."

"It's a long day's ride. Dead Horse is on the river due south of the foothills of the Superstition Mountains."

"Much obliged for the information and good luck to you!"

"Miners sure can use some good luck out here. Luck and a strong back."

Sutton rode out of the settlement, heading east, and, in his eagerness to reach Dead Horse which had been growing within him during the past several days, continued traveling through the heat of the day.

The clouds above him were turning red in the rays of the setting sun when he first saw the town spread out on the desert floor and the clouds were purple when he finally rode into Dead Horse.

He rode slowly down the only street in the town until he came to a general store with mining implements and lanterns displayed in its one window. He dismounted in front of it and, once inside, looked around until his eyes fell on the locked glass case in one dim corner.

He went over to it and was bending down to examine the guns on display when a voice from behind him said, "Can I be of service, sir?"

Without turning around, Sutton tapped an index finger on the case and said, "I'd like to take myself a look at that .44 Smith & Wesson Army revolver."

"Certainly, sir." The clerk rounded the case, unlocked it, and handed Sutton the revolver.

Sutton hefted it and sighted along its barrel.

"Fine single-action, top-break gun," the clerk declared enthusiastically.

"What're you asking for it? But wait a minute. Before you quote me a price, I should tell you that there's a whole flock of other things I'm in sore need of. A cartridge belt. Ammunition and a holster for this gun. A bedroll. A knife, flint, and steel. Some provisions. A good rifle and a leather saddle scabbard to carry it in. With a tall order like that, I bet you could give a good overall price, couldn't you?"

"Of course, sir. Definitely. Yes. I can make some adjustments to the prices of each individual item so that I'm sure you will be satisfied with the overall cost of your order—and I'm sure I can supply your needs. We receive regular shipments of the finest merchandise from Tucson and have even begun receiving goods from Phoenix which, as you may know, is already quite an active little center of commerce."

Fifteen minutes later, as Sutton paid for his purchases, he asked, "You been in business here long?"

"Almost two years," the clerk responded.

"Then I reckon you wouldn't know anything about an Apache attack on some settlers that took place just west of here twenty years ago."

The clerk shook his head.

"I need to find out anything I can about that raid. Which bunch of Indians pulled it off. Where they went after it. That sort of thing."

"I'm afraid I can't help you on that score, sir. Sorry."

"Maybe you can—if you can tell me who in town might happen to know something—anything—about that raid."

"Well, there's Lem Fennel. He's a real old-timer. He's been here—I don't know exactly how long actually but, I believe, a number of years. He might be able to help you."

"Where can I find him?"

"He's been known to spend a goodly amount of time in the Paradise Saloon. It's right across the street."

"Much obliged."

Sutton picked up his purchases. The Smith & Wesson rested in a Mexican-loop holster which hung from the Prairie cartridge belt strapped around his hips. He fastened the rifle scabbard to his saddle and slipped the Winchester .44 carbine into it. After tying his bedroll behind the cantle of his saddle, he led the dun across the street and looped its reins around the hitch rail in front of the Paradise Saloon.

Once inside, he looked around, disappointed to find the place empty except for the white-aproned and sleeve-gartered man behind the bar who was polishing glasses.

Sutton strode up to the bar and ordered whiskey.

When he had been served, he said, "I'm looking for a man named Lem Fennel. You know where I can find him?"

"Sure, I do," replied the bar dog. "He lives up over the tin shop down the street."

Sutton dropped a coin on the bar and downed his whiskey.

"But finding him isn't likely to do you much good," the bar dog added.

"Why's that?"

"Lemuel's been on a bender for near to a week now. And when he goes on one there's no talking sense to the man. Lemuel sees sights that aren't there. He raves like a man gone mad."

Sutton considered the information he had just been given and then said, "What I want to know from Lem is something maybe somebody else around here might be able to tell me."

"What do you want to know?" the bar dog asked in a suspicious tone of voice, his eyes appraising Sutton.

"Heard about an Apache raid that took place west of town twenty years ago. A boy was took in it. I'm trying to find him. You happen to know anything about which Apaches made that raid?"

"Nope. That was long before my time in town."

Sutton turned and started for the door.

"Hold on a minute, mister," the bar dog called out to him.

Sutton halted and turned to face the man.

"You ought to go talk to Miss Annie."

"Miss Annie?"

"That's the only name folks hereabouts know her by. She wandered into Dead Horse on foot when the town wasn't much more than a few wells and windmills. She'd been taken captive by some Apaches and she was a little the worse for wear, or so it's said. She hates redskins with a purple passion, Miss Annie does, and I guess she's got cause to."

"She lives here in town?"

"Down near the end of the street in a little adobe under an old aspen. You'll find her place easy, but I should warn you—she's a little loco."

"Much obliged."

Outside, Sutton stepped into the saddle and rode down the street until he came to the adobe that seemed to huddle beneath the sheltering arms of the ancient aspen.

He dismounted, went up to the door, and knocked.

"Leave me be!" cried a cracked voice from inside.

"I won't take too much of your time, Miss Annie," Sutton called out. "Just wanted to ask you a question or two."

"Don't know no answers to questions. Go away and leave me be!"

. . . she's a little loco.

The bar dog's words echoed in his mind. Sutton was about to call out again when a woman's head and shoulders suddenly appeared in the open window next to the door.

In her hands was an old rusted musket. She aimed it at Sutton and said, "I'll shoot the first Apache that tries to lay a hand on me."

Sutton quickly raised his hands above his head. "I'm no Apache, Miss Annie." He stared at her haggard face, meeting her lifeless eyes with a smile he hoped would gentle her as she studied him.

"Why, you're as white as me," she said softly.

"I told you the truth about me, Miss Annie."

"I shoot to kill Apaches," she muttered grimly.

"I guess you've got good reason to hold a grudge against them."

Miss Annie's dull eyes suddenly flared in fury. "Bastards!"

"They're no friends of mine neither."

"They took everything from me," Miss Annie murmured, lowering her musket.

Sutton slowly lowered his hands, the smile still fixed on his face.

"They even took my last name," Miss Annie continued, her old eyes glazed as she stared past Sutton. "Maybe my first one, too, though I do seem to remember my pa and ma calling me 'Annie.' My good name they took. I know they did. Why else did folks in town treat me so terrible when I came here—calling me 'squaw' and worse. But it weren't my fault what happened to me."

Sutton waited.

"I was clever," Miss Annie announced proudly a moment later, a sly smile spreading across her face to reveal broken and missing teeth. "Some weren't."

"What do you mean?" Sutton asked her, perplexed.

"I escaped."

Sutton, momentarily at a loss for the proper way to proceed, said nothing.

"Some didn't."

"Escape?"

"I took him with me but he was so little and he was soon all wore out. He fell back. I saw them catch him . . .

"I liked that boy. Just a little feller he was and as sweet as applesauce. He didn't remember nothing about how he'd got to the Apache camp. All he remembered was the name of this here town. So when the two of us ran off we headed here to see if we could find his folks. But the

Apaches caught him and took him back with them. *I* escaped." Miss Annie beamed at Sutton.

"You're telling me—you knew a boy who was taken in the raid that took place west of Dead Horse twenty years ago?"

Miss Annie shook her head in disgust. "How would I know where they took the boy from? Even he didn't know."

"But you said he knew the name of this town."

"That don't prove he was took near here."

"What was his name, Miss Annie?"

"He never would tell me though I asked, not that it matters much."

"Why doesn't it matter?"

"They took his real name away from him the same as they took mine. He ended up being called Two Drums. The Apaches called me Red Moon because of the color of my hair." Miss Annie proudly patted her gray hair. " 'Hair as red as a winter sunset,' my pa used to say I had."

"Which band of Apaches had you and the boy, Miss Annie?" Sutton asked in a gentle voice, hope stirring within him.

"Don't remember who they were and don't want to remember either. Do remember though that that bloodthirsty Geronimo was one of them. Folks say he's been killing whites all across the country of late."

Sutton managed to suppress the excitement that was growing within him. "Well, Miss Annie, I'd best be on my way now," he said evenly and picked up the trailing reins of his dun.

"You're setting out after Apaches?"

"I am."

"They'll have your hair if'n you ain't careful," Miss Annie warned.

"I'll try real hard to hold onto it."

Sutton stepped into the saddle and was about to touch the brim of his hat to Miss Annie, but she and her musket were gone from the window.

He rode out of Dead Horse, heading northeast, wondering if the boy Miss Annie had known, the one who had known the name of the town of Dead Horse, was in reality Vernon Adams. It was possible, he thought, although he knew that Miss Annie had been right when she had pointed out to him that the mere fact that the captive boy had known the name of the town of Dead Horse proved nothing. Still, it was a lead worth following up. More important, it was the only lead he had which might lead him to Vernon Adams or, at least, to some information about the man. Though it very well might not, he thought ruefully.

He intended to talk to Geronimo about the boy, so he continued riding northeast toward the reservation where Geronimo was, he knew, now confined.

Just before sunset that night, he spotted a mule deer in the distance and brought it down with a single shot from his carbine. He built a fire and then made a meal of venison roasted over the flames. Afterward, he cut thin strips of meat from what remained of the carcass and draped them over the branches of a leafless ocotilla to dry.

In the morning, after packing away the jerky, he rubbed down the dun with his saddle blanket before saddling and bridling it.

As he rode on and the day grew older, he left the Lower Colorado Valley behind him and moved into the uplands where the riding was alternately difficult and easy because of the rugged mountain chains and intermittent broad valleys he had to cross.

The slopes of the mountains were thick with paloverde

and mesquite and the valleys were spiked with furry cholla, barrel cactus, and prickly pear cactus. The sun streamed down on both the mountain ranges and the flat valleys between them and he sweated beneath it although he confined his daytime travel to the mornings and evenings.

At night, as the dun traveled over the mountains and across the valleys where the saguaros loomed like menacing enemies, with their thick arms raised and ready to do battle, the air was cooler and the land was alive with the sounds of scuttling and scurrying nocturnal creatures.

On the third day of his journey as a screech owl peered at him from its home in a tall saguaro and a white-winged dove flew over his head, Sutton spotted wickiups and adobe buildings sprawled on both banks of the Gila River. He galloped toward them, eager to ask the questions which were on his mind and which, once answered, might mean an end to his quest.

As he rode in among the buildings beside which Apaches squatted as they watched him wordlessly, he hailed the first white man he saw.

"Where's the agent located?" he asked as he rode up to him.

"There," replied the man, pointing to one of the adobe buildings.

Sutton rode over to it, dismounted, and, leaving the dun's reins trailing, entered the building.

"You the agent for the reservation?" he asked the middle-aged man who was counting blankets piled haphazardly against one wall.

The man gave Sutton a glance. "I am. My name is Charles Landell. And you are—"

"Name's Luke Sutton. I'm looking for Geronimo. Want to have a talk with him."

"What about?"

"I'm looking for a boy—he'd be a man grown by now—who was captured by Apaches twenty years ago west of the Gila River town of Dead Horse. I've learned that he lived with Geronimo and the Mimbreños, so it seemed to me that Geronimo ought to be able to tell me what happened to him—maybe where he is now—if he's still alive."

"Tracking white captives can be a thoroughly frustrating business," Landell remarked with a frown. "Many have never been found, although handsome ransoms have been offered in a number of cases. Some who've been located have refused to return to white civilization. Is the man a relative of yours?"

"Nope. He's the brother of a lady who hired me to find him if I can. You don't happen to have such a man here on the reservation by any chance, do you?"

Landell shook his head.

"Where's Geronimo?"

"He and the men who are loyal to him are—come with me."

The agent went to the door and pointed across the river to a low mountain range in the distance. "They're camped up there. There's a pass—you can just make it out from here. Follow it and you'll find them."

"Much obliged."

"That is, if they're still there."

Sutton, who was walking toward his dun, turned and looked back at the agent. "You mean you're expecting them to go back to the blanket?"

"It's a distinct possibility. As you may or may not know, Geronimo and his people have been here on the reservation before and they have fled. The man seems unable to make up his mind whether to stay here and live or return to their old world which is, as I'm sure they must realize, rapidly vanishing from the face of the earth."

"Well, I'd best be hurrying then," Sutton said. "I wouldn't want to miss meeting up with Geronimo after I've come such a long way to talk to him." He swung into the saddle, rode around the clustered wickiups and adobe buildings and then into the river.

When he reached the foothills of the mountain range, he rode into the pass and followed its sloping path upward for nearly a mile before the pass first broadened and then finally ended. Before Sutton was a sheltered valley in which a number of wickiups circled a communal cooking fire.

Gripping the reins in one hand, Sutton patted the neck of the dun and told it, "Let's go beard the lion in his den, old fellow." He moved the animal forward and rode out into the open.

The village, which had been alive with the sounds of men calling out to one another, babies crying, and dogs barking, suddenly fell silent. The Apaches stopped what they had been doing to turn and stare at Sutton as he approached them.

With his free hand, he pointed to himself and then held up his first two fingers, his other fingers and thumb folded against his palm in the sign for friend. Then he quickly made the signs for "work" and "with" to signify that he wanted help.

"Geronimo," he said aloud.

None of the Apaches moved. None spoke.

"Geronimo," he said a second time and this time one of the men stooped down and entered a wickiup.

He emerged moments later followed by a man of medium height who halted just outside the wickiup and stood with his arms folded, gazing up at Sutton.

"Geronimo," said the second man and pointed to himself.

Sutton quickly took in the Apache leader's fierce countenance—the overhung brows, outthrust cheekbones, and a hawk's nose above a straight, thin mouth.

"Anybody here know any English?" Sutton asked, his eyes sweeping the crowd.

The man who had summoned Geronimo raised his right hand, holding it flat with his palm outward at the height of his shoulders. He moved it in Sutton's direction and then brought it down.

Sutton nodded his willingness to wait and the Indian disappeared in the crowd of villagers.

He didn't have to wait long. When the Indian returned several minutes later, there was a man with him. Like his companion, he wore white cotton trousers that were tucked into knee-high buckskin leggings and a white blouse which was bound about his waist by a blue sash. His rugged face was almost as dark as that of the Apache beside him and his clear eyes were the color of roasted acorns. His hair, the pale shade of early morning sunlight, was straight and nearly shoulder length.

"You speak English?" Sutton asked the white man.

"I do. I also speak the Apache language. I've lived among these people for many years. My friend, Black Tree, tells me that you want to speak to Geronimo. I shall be happy to translate for you."

"My name's Luke Sutton—"

The man stepped up to the dun and held out his hand to Sutton who shook it. "My name is Wayne Chandler."

"I'd be obliged, Chandler, if you'd tell Gokhlayeh that I've come here to ask him about a white boy who was taken captive by the Apaches twenty years ago near the town of Dead Horse on the Gila River. The Apaches called the boy Two Drums, I'm told."

Sutton saw the surprise on Geronimo's face, the result, he supposed, of his having used the Apache leader's true name. There was an expression of surprise as well on Chandler's face.

Chandler looked away and translated Sutton's request for Geronimo.

Geronimo, his black eyes still on Sutton, spoke in a guttural tone to Chandler, who turned to Sutton and said, "He says he remembers Two Drums."

Sutton, exultant, wanted to let out a whoop of pure joy. Instead, he controlled himself and asked, "Where's Two Drums now?"

When Chandler had translated his question, his spirits sank as Geronimo, instead of responding to Chandler, merely shook his head and shrugged.

"Don't he know?" Sutton asked Chandler. "Or won't he tell?"

Chandler spoke again to Geronimo and Geronimo replied with a single word.

Chandler turned back to Sutton. "He does not know the whereabouts of Two Drums. The boy, it seems, ran away."

"When?" Sutton asked sharply. A moment later he had his answer from Geronimo via Chandler, "Twelve moons from the time Geronimo and his people captured him."

Sutton hesitated, not sure of his next move, and then he asked, "Find out for me, if you can, where the Apaches were when Two Drums escaped from them."

Geronimo's answer to the question was relayed through Chandler: "They were on the trail but had camped for several days under the Mogollon Rim."

Sutton told Chandler to ask if Geronimo had ever seen the boy again and was told that he had not.

Geronimo suddenly spoke.

— "He wants to know," Chandler said to Sutton, "what the boy means to you—if he is a relative of yours."

Sutton shook his head and explained that he was trying to find out if the boy had lived or died and, if he had lived, where the man he now would be could be found.

Geronimo spoke again after hearing Chandler's translation, his tone harsh, his eyes stony.

"He says that the boy may have died in the desert," Chandler told Sutton. "He says you may find, not the boy, but his bones."

"Maybe so," Sutton muttered, his former high spirits dashed. He released his reins. He raised both hands, palms down, fingers extended and swept them outward toward Geronimo and then down.

Geronimo's face remained impassive, showing not the slightest acknowledgment of Sutton's silent expression of thanks for the information he had been given.

Sutton had turned his dun and was about to ride away when Chandler called his name. He halted and, when Chandler came up to him, stared down at the man who, he thought, could easily be mistaken for an Apache himself were it not for the blond color of his hair.

"It's an unfortunate habit the Apaches had—kidnapping white children," Chandler remarked, looking up at Sutton. "But you must understand that they usually treated those children quite well. They even came to love many of them as their own, over the years."

"I like a man who sticks up for his friends."

Chandler's face darkened and he retorted defensively, "I'm proud to call the Apache my friends. They're a fine people and I've lived with them long enough to have learned to respect them and their ways—well, most of them."

"You work for Landell, do you?"

"No. I'm here on the reservation as a representative of the Light of the Lord Mission which is headquartered in Phoenix. I try to do what I can for the Indians. They have a difficult life here. Too little food and what food there is is far from the best. Whites ride onto the reservation and sell them whiskey which drives them crazy and causes them all kinds of trouble. Ranchers drive cattle up here to sell, and they see to it that the animals drink their fill from the Gila River before they're allowed to cross so that what the agent actually buys is a great deal of what the Indians call 'ghost meat.'"

"I appreciate your taking the time and trouble to help me out back there, Chandler."

"Glad to do it." Chandler hesitated a moment and then asked, "How did you know that Geronimo's real name was Gokhlayeh?"

"I hear things on the trails I travel. Remember some of them."

Chandler smiled and looked off into the distance. "I don't know why that Mexican yelled 'Geronimo' in the middle of that battle with the Apaches years ago. But it stuck to Gokhlayeh. It means Jerome."

He looked back at Sutton and said, "I wish you Godspeed in your search."

Sutton nodded to Chandler and then heeled the dun and rode out of the village.

He headed northwest through the mountains, hoping as he rode that he would find not the bones of the boy Vernon Adams had once been but maybe the man himself, given time. In the meantime, if he was lucky, he might learn some word of his whereabouts if Adams had managed to survive after his escape from the Apaches nineteen years earlier.

CHAPTER 6

Early in the morning of the first day after he left Geronimo's campsite on the reservation, Sutton, wearing his slicker, rode through a heavy rain that drenched his dun and the desert.

As his journey continued, he completed his crossing of the Natanes Plateau and arrived at the Salt River which he followed, still heading northwest.

The green-barked paloverdes were alive with bright yellow blossoms and the ocotillas were no longer barren bundles of thorny sticks but instead, as a sudden result of the rain, thick with young leaves that shimmered in the sun.

And in response to the nourishing rain, desert dandelions were blooming, mixed in a random riot of striking color with yellow poppies and purple owlclover.

Moths flew among the sharp green leaves of the banana yuccas, unmindful of the fact that they were fertilizing the plants which would in time, as a result of their efforts, burst into stately white bloom.

Sutton smiled as he rode on. Some folks figure, he thought, that the desert's a dead thing. They're wrong. It's as full of life as a pup having its ears pulled.

As if to prove his point, a roadrunner, the tuft on the top of its head down and a dead rattler in its beak, dashed across his path and disappeared in the underbrush.

Minutes later, a swarm of queen butterflies flitted

around and above him, their white-speckled orange and black wings propelling them through the dry air as they descended upon a brilliant carpet of gold fields where they perched, their wings flicking open and then shut, to feed on the flowers' nectar.

Later, Sutton found a suitable place to ford the river. When at last he reached the southernmost foothills of the Mogollon Mountains he found them a succession of ranges and basins, deeply gouged in places by long-vanished streams that had once flowed down to feed the Salt River behind him.

He thought as he rode that this was a vast and empty land he found himself in and he began to wonder if he were on a fool's errand. Vernon Adams might be anywhere—if he was still alive. He might have long ago fled the region and the Apaches.

He could be in St. Louis. Even Canada. Or married to some señorita and raising kids down in Mexico.

Sutton deliberately set these speculations aside, valid though he knew them to be, because they were not the kind of thoughts likely to keep him on the trail. Rather they were the kind of thoughts far more likely to slow him down, maybe even stop him. At best, they were certain to set him wondering, as he was doing at the moment, whether he was chasing a wild goose that would elude him in the end.

It was late in the afternoon when he rode up and out of a basin that was thick with ironwood and found himself facing the sheer wall of tall rock that was the Mogollon Rim. Even from his lofty elevation he had to look up to where it seemed to end only inches from the sky.

Well, he thought, here I am, and all on account of Geronimo said that him and his Apaches had been camped below the Rim when Adams escaped from them. Not, he thought, a whole helluva lot to go on.

He looked off to the right at the uninhabited land that was littered with sand, creosote bushes, and cacti. He turned his head to the left and saw the same empty vista lying in the purple shadows cast by the sun, now halfway below the western end of the Rim.

He spoke to the dun and it started down the slope and, when it reached the basin at the foot of the Rim, he laid his right rein against the animal's neck and the horse moved off to the left.

As Sutton rode through the shadows and the time passed, he found himself more than once scanning the ground on both sides of him. But he saw only the bones of what had once been a bobcat, no others.

He turned the dun and rode back to the point from which he had started.

There he halted his horse and sat his saddle, gazing at nothing, thinking of Adams, wondering what to do next.

He made up his mind. He dismounted and, leading the dun, began to climb the steep and rocky incline which would take him to the top of the Rim.

Nearly an hour had passed when he finally emerged after his hazardous climb and stood on top of the Rim.

In the west, the sun was descending so he decided to spend the night where he was. He was about to strip the gear from his horse when something about the sun attracted his attention.

The giant red ball was streaked vertically as it hung low in the sky. By a cloud?

Sutton had never seen a cloud so thin, so straight.

Smoke.

He swung into the saddle and rode toward what turned out to be a campfire. He halted the dun and halloed the campsite, causing the lone man hunkered down with his back to Sutton to leap to his feet and raise the rifle he had in his hands.

A moment later the man lowered the rifle, gestured, and Sutton rode up to the fire.

"I tend to get spooked, all alone out here," the man, who was bearded and grimy, told him. "The desert can do that to a man."

"It can," Sutton agreed. "You from around here?"

"Got a little place just south of the Little Colorado River. You?"

"Me? Well, you could call me a wandering man. At the moment, I'm hunting a man who was took captive by the Apaches twenty years ago and was last seen by them down below there." Sutton pointed to the edge of the Rim.

"I can't help you on that score," the man said, hunkering down again beside his fire. "What you ought to do is you ought to talk to Bill Chase."

"Why?"

"Chase has been round and about here for years. He's a regular old desert rat. Maybe he could tell you something you might like to know."

"Where can I find Chase?"

"He holes up in a shack due east of here. You ride along the Rim and pretty soon you'll come to a stream that runs north to the Little Colorado. Chase's place is right on that stream."

"Much obliged."

"You want some coffee, stranger? Got some cooking on the coals."

"Nope, but it's real nice of you to offer me some. I'd best find Chase's place before it gets dark."

Sutton turned the dun and, although he knew the animal was as tired as he himself was, he galloped east, the long shadows of saguaros stretching out before him as if pointing out the way to him.

He had begun to think he might have missed Chase's shack when the dun quickened its pace and he thought, this horse of mine smells water.

They came upon the stream several minutes later and the sturdy shack that sat less than a hundred yards from it.

Sutton slowed the dun, halted it, and called out, "Bill Chase!"

In response to his shout, an old man appeared in the open doorway, an expression of curiosity on his lined face.

"You lost?" he asked.

"Nope."

The man abruptly vanished inside the shack. Several moments later, he reappeared, a frown on his weathered face. "You aiming to sit that saddle of yours till the kingdom comes?"

"I don't usually step down 'less I'm asked to."

"Well then, step down. I reckon I'd best ask you to come on inside, too, else you'll be billeted on my door stoop for days."

Sutton, grinning, got out of the saddle, led the dun to the stream where he left it, and then followed the old man inside the shack. His first impression was one of a spicy darkness, the result of the dimness of the room and the food cooking in a kettle which hung from an iron hook above the flames in the fireplace.

"You come just in time to eat," the man remarked. "Set yourself down there"—he pointed to a crate beside the wooden table—"and I'll be about putting the finishing touches to this here chili."

He took down a cannister from a wall shelf and sprinkled something into the chili. He stirred the kettle's contents with a wooden spoon, tasted it, clucked his approval, and proceeded to spoon it onto a tin plate which he placed on the table in front of Sutton.

Sutton picked up a wooden spoon and began to eat. He almost spat the first spoonful of chili from his mouth.

The old man cackled mirthfully. "Hot stuff, huh?"

As Sutton managed to swallow the chili, he nodded, tears forming in his eyes. Then, as the old man left the room, he gingerly tried a second spoonful of the chili.

He got it down and was going, as gingerly, for a third when the old man reappeared, holding a dipper which he handed to Sutton.

"Rain water from the barrel outside," he told Sutton, who drank eagerly. "That rain we had a couple of days ago near filled the barrel and left behind a great big rainbow to boot. You see it?"

"I was way south of here two days ago."

"Too bad. Desert rainbows're as rare as courage in a coon." He bent down and opened the door of an oven built into the stone chimney. "Here," he said and dropped a biscuit on Sutton's plate. "They're safe. Didn't put so much as a speck of red pepper in *them.*" He cackled happily.

Later, after both men had finished eating, he announced, "I'm Bill Chase."

"Figured you were. Met a man on the trail who told me where to find you. My name's Luke Sutton. You lived here long, Chase?"

"I have, if you consider thirty years long."

"How'd you survive out here in the desert so long?"

"Almost as easy as turning a pumpkin into a pie. When I was young, I caught mustangs. Broke 'em. Sold 'em off. After that, I did me some prospecting. Made me some money I'm still using to get by on."

"You run into any trouble with the Apaches?"

"Some. Held my own though, I did. They're a bunch of roamers, those Injuns. Never light in one place for very long. Did I tell you I was in the cavalry? Learned to shoot real good on both horse and foot during my hitch in the Army. The Apaches, when they found that out, left me mostly alone."

"Chase, you might be able to help me out."

"Me? What can an old coot like me do to help out a strong-shouldered young buck like yourself?"

"I happen to know that Geronimo once camped in this neighborhood." Sutton proceeded to explain to Chase that he was searching for Vernon Adams.

Chase was silent as he considered the information. And then, "Twenty years ago, you say? It used to be I had a neighbor name of Hardy ten miles upstream twenty years back. Kept chickens, he did. Used to think, he told me once, that some kind of critter was stealing 'em. He used to find their bones and feathers not far from his place. But one night Hardy stood watch near his coop and he damn near blasted a dirty half-wild boy to bits."

"Vernon Adams, was it?" Sutton asked eagerly.

"Couldn't say. That boy spoke nary a word, to hear Hardy tell it at the time. He just made sounds like nothing human Hardy'd ever heard before. Got away, the kid did. Bit Hardy on the wrist and lit a shuck."

"You know what happened to the boy?"

"I know he stopped stealing Hardy's chickens."

"You figure he left the neighborhood."

"Sure, I do."

"And that was the last Hardy ever saw of him."

Chase shook his head. "You sure do take a lot for granted, Sutton. I never said that was the last Hardy ever saw of him."

"You didn't?"

"Like me, Hardy used to do some prospecting. He used to wander here and there looking for gold, silver, what-have-you. Well, once not long after his chickens stopped disappearing Hardy was down in the Superstition Mountains and he told me he put up at the shack of another prospector who let him lie the night on his floor one time and there the boy was all washed up and wearing near-clean clothes."

"Adams?"

"Damnation, Sutton! I never said it was the boy *you're* after. How would I know if he was? I already told you he didn't speak a word to Hardy. All I know is the prospector told Hardy he'd come upon the young 'un just this side of death's door and he took him in, nursed him, got him up on his own two feet again. 'Course it could have been this here Adams fellow. I'm not saying it wasn't anymore'n I'm saying it was on account of I can't."

"Was he a brown-haired boy?"

"Hardy didn't say and I never laid an eye on the kid myself."

"I wonder, Chase, could you tell me how to find this prospector's shack where Hardy saw the boy."

"Twenty years is a long time," Chase mused. "That prospector—"

"What was his name?"

"Hardy called him Matt's all I know. I don't know if Hardy knew his last name or not. He just called him Matt. Yes, sir, like I said, twenty years is a long time. That Matt could be long gone by now. Sometimes I wonder why I'm still around, seeing as I'm pushing eighty real hard. But I used to do a lot of drinking in my younger days. The red-eye's probably got me so pickled I keep."

As Chase's cackle filled the room, Sutton reached out

and gripped the old man's arm. When Chase was silent once more, he repeated, "Could you tell me how to find that prospector's shack?"

"Sure I could on account of Hardy mentioned its whereabouts to me." Chase proceeded to give Sutton directions.

As Sutton got up from the table, he said, "I appreciate your hospitality, Chase."

"You're moving on? Right now?"

Sutton nodded.

"You're not. You'll stay the night."

Sutton glanced through the open door into the young evening.

"You owe me for that meal I fed you," Chase said, "even though it did almost set you afire."

"I've got money. I'll gladly pay you."

"I don't want money. I want you."

"Me?"

"To talk to. To sit with for a spell. It gets lonelier out here than a cowboy who didn't skip out of the way of a skunk fast enough." Chase glared at Sutton. "You'll stay the night?"

"I will."

"Good," Chase said and slapped both of his knees. "I'll tell you all about the time—near to a whole year, it was—that I spent right here in this shack with a young Apache girl who tried her damndest to marry me!"

Sutton, grinning, left the shack and went outside to see to his horse.

That's them, Sutton told himself days later as he rode south across the desert, which was covered with towering saguaros, the tops of their branches thick with waxy white blossoms. His eyes were on the looming peaks, buttes, and pillars of rock containing countless canyons that were the Superstition Mountains just ahead of him.

Later, as he rode through a deep draw, he welcomed the relative coolness after the punishing heat of the desert. Here in the mountains he found piñons and junipers, and the trees shed welcome shade upon him and his horse. As he climbed higher, he found himself riding through a ponderosa pine forest, with shadows and a hawk that soared high in the bright blue sky his only companions.

But his solitude did not last as he rounded a ragged outcropping of rock and suddenly came upon two men and a woman who were seated around a dead fire. Two horses and two loaded pack mules stood near them.

Sutton's Smith & Wesson cleared leather as one of the men, moonfaced and thick-lipped, leaped to his feet and went for the Dance revolver that was stuck in his waistband.

"I'll drop you if you draw that gun," Sutton told the man.

The moonfaced man's lips parted and words slid between them, words Sutton didn't catch.

"Beg pardon?"

"I said you followed us up here," the moonfaced man told Sutton.

"You're wrong, mister. I'm not trailing you. I'm looking for the place where a miner name of Matt used to live some years back here in these mountains."

"Jacob," said the second man as he rose to his feet, "maybe he's telling the truth."

The woman, an Apache, stared silently at Sutton.

"Wisner," said the man named Jacob, "you know that every sonofabitch in Phoenix is trying to find out where—"

Wisner seized Jacob's arm to silence him and succeeded in doing so.

"I'll be moving on now," Sutton said evenly. "If you folks'll just let me pass peaceable like, we'll all be fine. You don't—you try to down me—you're dead. I see you only got one gun to the three of you."

"Let him pass, Jacob," Wisner advised, and the moon-faced man stepped back, his lips working soundlessly.

Sutton moved the dun forward and to the right, his finger on the trigger of his .44.

"We didn't mean to cause you any trouble," Wisner said. "This man is my friend. His name is Jacob Walzer. We're partners. The lady is his woman."

"Your friend Walzer," Sutton said, "could learn a lesson from his lady—how to keep quiet and not go shooting his mouth off at every stranger he happens to run into."

Wisner laughed nervously. "You may well be right about that. But in the case of his woman—well, she's got no choice. Her people tore her tongue out."

"We might consider doing that to you," Walzer barked at Sutton. "If you keep following us."

"Told you I wasn't following—"

Sutton's words were cut off by the ugly *ping-ping* of a carbine fired from somewhere nearby. He was out of the saddle and down behind a rock formation in seconds as Walzer, Wisner, and the woman scurried to find similar cover.

Rounds from two carbines fired almost simultaneously bit into the ground close to where Sutton crouched behind his rocky breastwork, his revolver in his hand.

He squeezed off a shot, aiming high at the point from which he had seen the shots fired.

When his fire was returned, he squeezed off another round which sent splinters of rock flying into the air.

Across from him and more than half hidden by a cluster of small boulders, Walzer, wide-eyed, was scanning the walls of rock, obviously searching for whoever was attacking the campsite.

Sutton, the hammer of his .44 thumbed back, also scanned the high rocks but saw no one.

Not at first.

But then a head appeared. And then hands holding an Army carbine.

"Get down!" Sutton shouted as the Apache aimed his carbine at Walzer.

Walzer dropped down behind the boulders as Sutton fired once.

The Apache rose to his knees. His arms trembled and his body shuddered. The carbine fell from his hands. He pitched forward and bounced down the sloping side of the rock wall to hit the boulders Walzer was hiding behind.

Sutton ran crouching, keeping his body bent, and then, as he came out into the open, he zigzagged across the ground until he reached an outcrop of rock which he ducked under. He eased along the curving wall of rock until he was sure he was out of sight of the one remaining gunman.

One?

Maybe more, he thought, as he holstered his gun and scrambled up the rocky wall, his feet slipping and his hands beginning to bleed where the jagged rocks sliced into them.

When he came to a narrow ledge, he sprawled upon it, drew his gun, and took aim at the Apache opposite him. The Indian was about to fire on Walzer who was standing up in plain sight now, looking down at the dead Apache lying broken on the boulders, a broad smile on his round face.

Sutton let out a wordless yell.

His tactic worked.

The Apache, distracted, turned and fired at him.

The bullet struck just below the ledge on which Sutton lay spread-eagled.

With both hands on his gun, he squeezed the trigger.

The Apache's body folded down upon itself. Losing his grip on his rifle he fell to the ground.

Sutton waited, not moving except to thumb back the hammer of his gun, his eyes on the unmoving body of the Apache.

When it did not stir after several minutes, he rose, holstered his .44, and climbed back down the rock wall, dislodging as he did so some stones which clattered down to the ground below.

On the level again, he wiped his bloody hands on his jeans, thumbed some cartridges from his belt, and inserted them into his revolver's empty chambers.

"You're some sure shot," Walzer told him grudgingly.

"You all right?" Sutton asked.

Walzer nodded. "Wisner, you can come out now. It's all over."

A moment later, Wisner emerged from around a bend in the high rock wall, followed by the Apache woman.

Sutton made his way to his dun which, during the shooting, had trotted to a position beyond Wisner and the woman.

"Where you going?" Walzer called out to him.

Sutton didn't answer. When he reached his horse and reached out to grip the reins, he noticed the ruins of an old Spanish smelter lying in the mouth of the cave where

Wisner and the Apache woman had evidently taken shelter when the shooting started.

Sutton peered into the cave, and despite its dim interior he was able to make out specks of gold lying on the ground near its entrance.

He led the dun back to where Walzer stood with the others and said, "I reckon you folks don't know you're on the Apaches' sacred ground. Those two I killed were Tonto Apaches and I reckon they didn't take too kindly to you folks stealing their thunder god's gold."

"I don't know what the hell you're talking about," Walzer growled.

"Is that a fact? Seems strange, you don't. Why, when I was still living over in Texas I heard talk about how Miguel Peralta, his son Pedro, and a whole passel of their miners were massacred by the Apaches on account of they were mining gold here in the Superstitions. Looks to me like you might have found the lost Peralta mine."

"I told you," Walzer snapped, "I don't know what you're talking about."

Sutton walked over to the nearest pack mule. He pulled his bowie knife from his boot and sliced into the roped tarpaulin on the animal's back.

Golden nuggets spilled from the rent in the bundle.

Sutton picked one up. It glinted in the sunlight as he said, "This here's what I'm talking about." He tossed it high into the air and Wisner ran forward, caught it, and hastily stuffed it into his pocket before beginning to scramble about on all fours to retrieve the nuggets that had fallen from the mule's pack.

"It's all pretty clear to me now," Sutton said. "When I first got here you accused me of following you. I see now that you figured I'd followed you to find out where the lost Peralta mine was. Your woman," he continued, addressing Walzer, "might have known where the Apaches' thunder god stored his gold. She might have gone and told you. Maybe that's why her people tore her tongue out.

"Well, I got to tell you something—all of you. You keep taking gold out of that mine and you're all likely to wind up massacred just like the Peraltas and their people were. But what you decide to do's none of my affair."

Sutton swung into the saddle and, without another word, rode away from the campsite.

When he finally came upon a shack where Chase said Matt's had been, he was happy to see signs of habitation. A hatchet's gleaming blade was partially buried in a chopping block near the door. A supply of firewood was piled beside one wall of the shack. On the opposite side of the building someone had hung a pair of woolen socks on a tree branch to dry.

Sutton called out, "Matt! You in there?"

A moment later, a middle-aged man, unshaven and unkempt, opened the door of the shack. "You're looking for Matt?"

"I'm glad to meet you," Sutton said sincerely.

The man shook his head. "I'm Red Bender."

"Where's Matt?"

"Get down off that horse and I'll take you to him."

Sutton dismounted and followed Bender around behind the shack where the man stopped and pointed.

"He's there," Bender announced.

Sutton walked past Bender and went up to the rotting wooden marker on which someone had burned the words HERE LIES MATT ALBRIGHT.

Sutton swore.

Bender came up beside him and said, "Seems kind of strange you're looking for Matt, considering he's been dead now nigh onto fifteen years. I took to partnering with him not long before he died."

Hope flared within Sutton. "Did he have a boy living with him then, do you recall?"

"He did. Said he'd caught him raiding this here very shack looking for food. That was some years before Matt and me met and took to partnering. He said the kid was as wild as any cougar at first. But Matt tamed him."

"What happened to the boy?"

"Don't know. He took off one day—the very day Matt died, as a matter of fact."

"Did he ever tell you his name? Where he was from? Anything at all like that?"

Bender shook his head. "Didn't talk much, that kid didn't. Matt told me he couldn't seem to remember anything about how he got to be running loose in the mountains up here, without no kin nor even any clothes. Matt said the kid was all cut up and bruised when he first trapped him. Had him, Matt said the kid did, a scar running right across his ribs. Matt never could find out how he got it. You'd ask the kid and he'd just stare at you with those big brown eyes of his that always looked sort of scared as if he'd spotted something awful and was wary of ever seeing the same sight again."

"Much obliged to you," Sutton said and swung into the saddle.

"Was the kid kin of yours?"

"Nope."

"You could ask around about him here in the mountains. They're chock full of old-timey prospectors like me."

"Much obliged, Bender," Sutton said and rode away, thinking that if he had any kind of good sense he'd do a little digging down in Walzer's mine before moving on.

But that old thunder god the Apaches have got might have my hair if I did, he thought. The old boy's not about to have his gold stolen and stand idly by. He'll keep his Tontos after the likes of Walzer and Wisner till they finish what they started out to do today.

As he rode on, he considered what little he had learned about Vernon Adams. It's not much, he thought, after all the wearying riding I've been doing. Adams, Bender said, has got brown eyes and a scar of some kind across his ribs. According to Mrs. Soames, he's got brown hair.

There are an awful lot of men with brown hair and eyes, he thought disgustedly. But not all that many with scarred ribs. Trouble is how'm I going to find this brown-eyed, brown-haired, rib-scarred mister when every trail I take trying to find him winds up a dead end?

Geronimo.

As the name resounded in Sutton's mind, he decided to have another talk with the man. And with, if possible, the Apaches who had been with Geronimo during the time they had held Adams captive. One of them might remember something that will point me in a new direction, he thought.

But if that don't work, he decided, I'll head on back to Dead Horse and have another try at talking to Miss Annie.

He let the dun under him pick its way around the debris left by a rockslide and then headed toward the reservation.

CHAPTER 7

Sutton, riding through a canyon, was startled by the sound of rifle and revolver fire as he approached Geronimo's camp.

He heard a woman scream. And then a man shout.

The firing continued as he drew rein and sat his saddle, listening and wondering what was happening up ahead of him. He could see nothing because the canyon through which he was riding curved to the left up ahead of him.

Sounds like one regular all-out war, he thought.

He turned the dun and headed back the way he had come until he reached the northern end of the canyon. Heeling his horse, he rode up to high ground and then along the rimrock until he was able to make out, despite the dust being raised by the horses of many mounted men, Geronimo's camp which was a roiling mass of men, both whites and Apaches, wailing women, some with babies in their arms as they fled seeking cover, and wildly barking dogs.

He got out of the saddle and then knelt upon the ground near the edge of the rimrock. He stared down at the melee below him, unable to tell whether the Apaches were attacking the white horsemen or whether the mounted men were attacking the Apaches.

Some of those whites are wearing galluses, he observed. One's got himself a dirty derby hat. The one perched on the bay gelding's wearing high-top shoes. They're not cowboys, he decided, not dressed like that they're not. There's not a single bandanna or a Stetson among them. Townsmen, he decided. But what are townsmen doing raising a ruckus here on the reservation? he wondered.

A stray shot whined over his head and he hugged the ground and removed his hat. Then, raising his head slightly, he looked down again just in time to see an Apache woman, who was running and holding a girl by one hand and a boy by the other, stumble and then fall. The two children with her ran on a few steps and then the boy turned and started back to where the fallen woman lay without moving, blood reddening the back of her blue cotton blouse.

A white rider raced after several fleeing Apaches. His horse leaped over the body of the woman on the ground and as it did, its left front hoof struck the boy who was standing frozen above the prone woman and he fell backward and hit the ground. As the horseman galloped on, the boy scrambled to his feet and began to run to where the girl now huddled behind the thick trunk of a ponderosa pine.

If she had been his destination, he never reached her. A bullet entered his right leg and, crippled by it, he hobbled on for several paces before dropping to his knees and beginning to crawl along the ground, leaving a trail of bright blood behind him.

A sudden steady volley of shots sounded and Sutton saw a furious battle between five armed white men on horseback and a lone Apache, his only weapon a skinning knife.

Just beyond the battling group, a man put a torch to a wickiup and it went up in crackling flames.

Sutton had seen enough. Clapping his hat back on his head, he leaped to his feet and let out a roar, attracting the attention of the men battling below him. At the same instant, he kicked out and booted a huge boulder that went careening over the edge of the canyon wall to scatter the surprised men who were standing momentarily immobile as they stared up at him in surprise.

Sutton's .44 cleared leather as one of the men raised a Spencer rifle and angled it up at him. Sutton's shot slammed into the rifleman's shoulder and he let out a yelp that was a blend of shock and anger.

Sutton booted another boulder over the canyon wall and then another even larger one, succeeding in separating the two warring factions if only temporarily.

"Now, you boys best not try scampering over those rocks after any Indians," he yelled. "The first one of you who does—"

"You got no part in this, mister," one of the whites he had addressed yelled up at him.

An Apache—the man with the skinning knife—leaped up onto one of the boulders. Brandishing his weapon, he was about to spring upon the rider nearest him.

Sutton sent a shot whizzing past the Apache, causing him to leap backward and fall to the ground on the side of the boulder away from the man he had been about to attack.

"I don't know the whys or wherefores of this fight," Sutton shouted, "but I do know that you men've got no right causing a commotion here on the reservation. I'm giving you just two minutes to ride right on out of here. You don't—and from up here where you'll have some trouble dropping me—I'll turn every last one of you into something even hell won't have."

Sutton stood his ground, wondering if his bluff—for that's what he knew it to be—would be called.

The men below him hurriedly consulted together, their horses circling, one rearing as sparks from the burning wickiup drifted past it on the breeze. They glared up at Sutton who glared right back at them.

Then, not wanting to give the riders any more time to think, he fired, sending a bullet close to the head of a horse that was directly below him which caused the animal to snort, buck, and almost throw its rider.

Sutton fired again and this time his shot sent a six-shooter careening from its owner's hand.

One of the riders suddenly swung around and went galloping south. Two others wheeled their mounts and followed him a moment later. Then all of them were riding rapidly out of the camp.

All except one. One who was, Sutton noticed for the first time, unarmed.

"You too, mister," he shouted at the man. "Move on out!"

The man astride the black looked up at Sutton and then he took off his hat.

Sutton recognized Wayne Chandler. He stepped back from the edge and reloaded his revolver. Then he got into the saddle and not long afterward rode up to Chandler who said, "Thanks for your help."

"Chandler, I have met a few foolhardy men in my time but you—well, you are without a doubt the foolhardiest I've laid eyes on so far."

Chandler's eyebrows rose in surprise.

"Right smack in the middle of the melee you were with no rifle, no sidearm, no nothing to help you hold your own."

"I'm a man of peace," Chandler said. "I—"

"What was a man of peace doing in the thick of that battle that just took place right here? Can you tell me that if you've time?"

"Well, I was coming back here from another part of the

reservation where I'd been preaching the Word and I
rode right into the fray, so to speak."

"You rode right into what could have been the end of
your preaching for good and all."

"I know," Chandler murmured sheepishly, "but I
couldn't just stand by and do nothing, could I?"

Sutton sighed. "What caused all the commotion and
whose side were you fighting on?"

"Those men rode in here claiming that some Apaches
raided their settlement south of the Gila River last week.
To answer your second question, I was fighting on the side
of the Apaches."

"Did your friends do what those men claimed they
did?"

"I don't know. I do know that those men had no right to
come here and . . ." Chandler fell silent. He looked
around and then waved one arm in an all-encompassing
gesture that included the dead and wounded Apaches
and the burning wickiup.

"I try not to be a troublesome man, Chandler, but if
somebody hits me, I hit him right back."

Chandler almost smiled.

"I'm not an educated man," Sutton added, "but I do
know there's two sides to every story."

"Sutton, these Apaches weren't armed, most of them.
Look around you. That woman—she's dead. That boy—
shot in the leg. Do you mean to tell me you endorse what
those men just did?"

Sutton ignored the question and walked over to where
the boy who had been wounded in the leg was sitting on
the ground beside the girl he had been fleeing with earlier. "We'll get you fixed up, boy," Sutton told him, doubt-
ing that the boy understood English. "Fixed up fine too."
As Sutton reached down, the boy shrank away from him.

Chandler came over and spoke words Sutton didn't understand. "I told him it's all right," he explained to Sutton. "I told him he needn't be afraid of you."

Sutton bent down and picked up the boy.

"Chandler!"

Sutton turned at the sound of the shout to find Charles Landell riding through the camp.

"Mr. Landell," Chandler said when the agent reached him, "I tried to stop the fight. I failed. But Luke did manage to run those riders off."

"Who were they?" Landell asked.

Chandler told him what he had earlier told Sutton.

"You and I, Chandler," Landell said, "are apparently wasting our time trying to civilize these savages."

"Excuse me, Mr. Landell," Chandler said, "but there is no proof that Geronimo's people—or any other Apaches here on the reservation—raided that white settlement."

"You think those men were lying then?"

"No, Mr. Landell, I'm not saying that. But—"

"I received word several days ago that Apaches raided the town of Twisted Tree and I took prompt action to insure that it would not happen again."

"Action?"

Sutton thought he had heard a tremor in Chandler's voice. He was sure that the expression on Chandler's face as he waited for Landell's answer was one of uneasiness, if not outright fear.

Landell cleared his throat and replied, "I sent word at once to Camp Apache about the raid and asked that a force of cavalry be sent here to help us keep the peace."

"To help us keep the peace," Chandler repeated sarcastically. "Or to punish the Apaches?"

"Chandler, may I remind you of something? You are here on the reservation through the sufferance of the

Indian Bureau. Now, I am willing to acknowledge that your work among the Apaches is not only well-intentioned but also of benefit to the Indians in my charge. However, I have a clear duty to see to it that the Indians remain on the reservation and an equally clear duty to see to it that they do not become marauders.

"But marauders they have become in at least one recent instance—that of Twisted Tree. Your presence here, Chandler, could be construed by some as one of giving aid and comfort to the enemy, offering them an implicit if unstated endorsement of their savage ways. Some might go so far as to say you are a decidedly disruptive influence on the reservation. That your presence here and your behavior are contrary to the government's aims and desires. Do I make myself understood?"

"Mr. Landell, I'm a missionary. I try to alleviate the lot of the Apaches, which is not a happy one as I believe you will admit. I have never intended to provoke trouble of any kind between the Apaches and white men."

" 'Intended,' I submit, Mr. Chandler, is the operative word. As for results, intended or not, well, that is another matter entirely."

"Landell," Sutton said, "I was up in the Superstitions not long ago and there are Tontos roaming around up there. Now who's to say a bunch of them didn't attack Twisted Tree?"

"No one, Mr. Sutton," Landell answered almost cheerfully. "But I'm afraid you're missing the point. The point is I intend to make certain none of *my* charges become involved in such attacks."

Sutton decided there was no use arguing with the agent, but he couldn't resist remarking, "This boy here went and got himself involved in an attack. He needs a doctor. You got one?"

"Yes. You'll find Dr. Esmond at the agency."

"You coming, Chandler?" Sutton shot over his shoulder as he carried the wounded boy to his dun.

"Not now, Luke. I'd better stay here."

Sutton placed the boy astride the dun and then swung up in front of him. He rode out of the camp and down through the pass toward the agency on the south bank of the Gila River.

After fording the river, he located Dr. Esmond's house easily enough and found Esmond ushering an elderly Apache out of his office.

"What's this?" Esmond asked, his eyes on the wounded boy as the old man limped out into the sunlight.

Sutton told him.

"Geronimo's camp was attacked?"

Sutton nodded.

"My surgery is this way."

As Esmond, followed by Sutton, entered the surgery, the doctor said, "There'll be hell to pay now. That's my guess. Geronimo won't sit still for his people being killed and wounded."

"Can't hardly blame the man for feeling put out, considering what happened," Sutton said as he placed the boy on Esmond's examining table.

The doctor was about to inspect the boy's leg when the boy pulled away from him and seized Sutton's hand with both of his own and gripped it tightly.

"Now, son," Esmond said, "I've got to have a look at you."

Sutton met the boy's frightened gaze. *"Coo-ee,"* he murmured and squeezed the boy's hands. "You just hang on to me, boy, and we'll see this here thing through together. *Coo-ee,"* he repeated softly.

Hesitantly, the boy allowed Esmond to examine his wounded leg, while still gripping Sutton's hand.

"You talk to my patient like he was a horse," Esmond commented as he began to clean the wound.

"Horses don't understand English," Sutton said. "I reckon he don't neither. But both him and horses understand somebody trying to be kind to them whatever language that somebody happens to be speaking."

Esmond gave Sutton a penetrating look and then said, "The bullet went through his calf. It didn't do too much damage. Hand me that bottle of antiseptic over there."

Sutton handed over the bottle and Esmond proceeded to sterilize the wound after which he bandaged it.

"That will do for now," he said, stepping back.

"Let's go, boy." Sutton picked up the patient, thanked the doctor, and left the surgery.

Once outside, he seated the boy on the dun and then swung into the saddle and headed back to the mountain camp.

When he reached it, he found the wickiup that had been put to the torch was now nothing but a pile of smoldering ashes from which thin wisps of smoke were rising. Women were weeping. Children stood about listlessly as if stunned. The dogs were silent, some of them asleep.

"Chandler!" Sutton called out and the missionary turned, saw him, patted the Apache he had been speaking with on the shoulder, and strode over to where Sutton was sitting his saddle.

"The doc patched up this here boy," Sutton told him. "You'll want to hand him over to his family."

"His mother was killed during the attack," Chandler said, his eyes on the boy. "But his sister's alive. I've arranged for both children to be taken in by another family."

Chandler spoke to the boy and then helped him down from the dun.

As Chandler carried the boy away, Sutton touched his horse's flanks with his boot heels and rode over to the wickiup from which he had seen Geronimo emerge during his previous visit to the camp. He got out of the saddle and stuck his head through the entrance to the wickiup.

Empty.

He straightened, turned, and surveyed the camp.

Geronimo was not in sight.

Dead?

But the bodies of the dead had been removed so Sutton couldn't be sure. He stood there, pulling thoughtfully at his stubbled chin. Then he picked up his reins and walked his horse to where Chandler stood with a group of Apaches who were embracing the wounded boy and whispering soft words to him while his sister stood silently nearby, tears turning her large eyes into black pools.

Sutton waited until the adults began to shepherd the children inside a wickiup and then he stepped up to stand beside Chandler. "I had no luck finding the Apache captive I'm hunting," he told the missionary.

"I'm sorry."

"Every trail I followed took me nowhere. The only thing I could think of to do was come on back here and have me another talk with Geronimo and any of his people who were with him when the Adams family was set upon—if any of them happen to be here now with Geronimo."

"I'm sorry," Chandler repeated, his eyes dull.

"Chandler?"

"Geronimo's gone."

"Gone? You mean he jumped the reservation?"

"He and some of the young men went to take revenge for the raid on their camp."

Sutton suppressed an oath. "Where were they headed, do you know?"

Chandler turned and met Sutton's gaze. "You intend to go after him?" When Sutton nodded, Chandler continued, "If you should find him—given the mood he's in—the bloodthirsty mood he's in—he'll undoubtedly kill you just as he will kill any other whites he comes upon."

"I've got to talk to him."

"And you called me foolhardy before."

"I don't see what else I can do, Chandler. There's almost no place else I can think of to turn to for information about Vernon Adams. Geronimo or one of his men might be able to tell me something that could help me find Adams."

"I'll tell you what else you can do, Luke. You can give up the search for Adams. If you go after Geronimo . . ." Chandler shrugged.

"I might manage to stay alive if I catch up with him. I'm not altogether ignorant of the ways of Apaches. I did some scouting for the Army once upon a time. Became friends with an Apache who was hired to do the same thing. Even spent some time with the Lipans down along the Pecos River with my Apache friend and the people of his village."

Sutton realized that Chandler wasn't listening to him. The man was staring off into the distance. He looked in the same direction and saw the Gila River and the cavalry who were fording it.

Chandler's voice, when he spoke, was low and unsteady. "You heard Landell say he sent word about the raid on Twisted Tree to Camp Apache. It does look as if he's gotten what he wanted. Armed might in the person of those cavalrymen who are coming this way. The sight of them makes me glad that Geronimo and his men are gone. Those soldiers would have treated them as criminals."

"You didn't answer the question I asked you, Chandler."

"Question?"

"Do you know where Geronimo's headed?"

"South. Into Mexico."

"He just might run into some trouble along the way. Unless he steers clear of towns. Unarmed, him and the men with him'll be easy pickings for—"

"They're not unarmed," Chandler interrupted.

"What say?"

"Geronimo had a cache of arms—Army carbines mostly —hidden away. He and his men retrieved them before they left the reservation."

"You knew this all along—about the guns?"

"I knew."

"And you never told anybody?"

Chandler shook his head defiantly. "My job here is to proselytize, not to inform on friends."

"Would the fact that Landell treats you like less than dirt have anything to do with you keeping your mouth shut about those guns?"

Chandler turned away without answering the question.

The sound of the troopers approaching caused Sutton to turn and watch their progress. The lieutenant leading the long line of paired men was young, he noted. He's younger than his right hand man, he thought, that sergeant of his who looks like his spine's melted so's he has to slump in the saddle. Not much older, the officer isn't, than those boys he's leading who look like they don't yet have need of a straight razor, most of them.

The lieutenant called a halt and spoke to the sergeant on his right.

The sergeant rode up to Sutton and Chandler. As he drew rein, he asked, "Is this Geronimo's camp?"

"It is," Chandler answered. He pointed. "That's his wickiup."

The sergeant nodded. "Agent Landell told the lieutenant that there was a preacher of some kind living here with the redskins. Which one of you—"

"I'm not a preacher," Chandler corrected the sergeant. "I'm a missionary from Phoenix."

"The lieutenant wants to have a word with you about giving him some help in keeping the redskins in line." The sergeant glanced at Sutton. "You a missionary too?"

"Nope."

"You belong here on the reservation?" the sergeant asked suspiciously.

"About as much as I belong anyplace, I reckon."

Chandler went over to where the lieutenant was sitting his horse at the head of his line of troopers, his gloved hands folded around his saddle horn.

The sergeant followed him and Sutton trailed along behind the sergeant.

"I'm Wayne Chandler," Chandler was saying as Sutton came up.

"Ah, Mr. Chandler," said the lieutenant. "Mr. Landell told me you would be of help to me in my efforts to pacify the Apaches here on the reservation who have, I'm given to understand, become rather boisterous of late. Allow me to introduce myself, if I may. Lieutenant Richard Nelson, sir. And this is Sergeant Petry." Nelson turned his attention to Sutton.

"Luke Sutton, Lieutenant. I'm just passing through."

Turning back to Chandler, Nelson said, "I have it in

mind to offer a system of small rewards for good behavior on the part of the Indians on the reservation. I believe in approaching difficult matters in a positive manner. Of course, as a corollary to the rewards there will also be established punishments for any infractions of the rules I intend to institute."

"You'll get no help from me," Chandler stated angrily.

"I beg your pardon, Mr. Chandler. I thought—"

"I don't give a damn what you thought, Lieutenant. I've seen enough—far too much—of the way we whites treat the Indians once we've moved in and taken over their land and their lives. Not only will you get no help from me enforcing the rules—whatever they might be—you intend to establish, but also I will do all I can to frustrate your efforts if, in my opinion, they are detrimental to the well-being—both physical and spiritual—of the Apaches in any way."

"Sir," said the sergeant, "it looks like the agent was right about this church mouse."

"Mr. Landell warned me," the lieutenant said to Chandler, "that you were not what might be called a benign influence here on the reservation. Apparently, he was quite correct. Well, let me tell you here and now that I intend to take immediate charge of matters and see to it that the Apaches learn not only to toe the line I shall draw for them but also learn to like toeing it."

"Lieutenant Nelson," Sutton said, "I'd like to put in a word or two, if that's all right with you, though I know that none of this is any of my business."

"What's on your mind, Mr. Sutton?"

"Well, Lieutenant, I reckon if you start out being too stiff with the Apaches you'll wind up with a reservation even emptier than it is now. Maybe you ought to try taking things a little bit slower, maybe even sort of soft at the start."

"Discipline is the answer in a situation like this, Mr. Sutton. Softness indicates weakness."

"Not necessarily, it don't."

"Mr. Sutton, what did you mean about my methods possibly making the reservation—I believe you said 'emptier than it is now'?"

"Geronimo's gone. So are some of his warriors."

"Gone where?" Petry asked. "And why?"

Chandler, smiling, replied, "They do not intend to let themselves be brutally attacked as they were this very day."

"Sergeant," Nelson said stiffly, "it is obvious that our first order of business is to bring Geronimo and his band back here."

"Lieutenant Nelson, are you familiar with this country —and the desert south of here?" Chandler inquired. "Are you experienced in the art of tracking Apaches who do not want to be found?"

"I must answer no to both of your questions, Mr. Chandler. I am executing my first command since graduating from the cadet corps of West Point. But I am familiar with the history of warfare, with approved military tactics—"

Chandler erupted in laughter, cutting off Nelson's speech, which had sounded to Sutton faintly arrogant as well as decidedly confident—perhaps too confident.

"I told you, Lieutenant Nelson," Chandler said when his laughter had subsided, "that I intend to frustrate your efforts to control the Apaches on the reservation."

"You did, but I am perfectly capable of dealing with you in whatever way may become necessary."

"Well, I've changed my mind."

"Ah, that is good news, Mr. Chandler. Good news indeed. I shall welcome your cooperation during our military rule of the reservation."

"I intend instead," Chandler said soberly, "to ride out of here right now. I intend to find Geronimo and warn him of your intentions to capture him."

Chandler turned swiftly and went to where his black stood beneath a scrub oak, tearing at its leaves.

Nelson barked an order to Sergeant Petry and Petry ordered a trooper to apprehend Chandler which the trooper promptly did, holding the missionary at bay with his Army Colt.

"Have that man taken to Mr. Landell at the agency," Nelson ordered the sergeant. "I want him imprisoned to prevent him from making contact with Geronimo."

Sutton watched as Chandler boarded his black and then rode out of the camp, with the trooper riding behind.

"That man," Nelson muttered. "One would think he would show more respect for a commissioned officer of the United States Army." Turning to Sutton, he asked, "Where did Geronimo and his companions go?"

Sutton thumbed his hat back on his head and, staring up at Nelson with a bland expression on his face, answered, "Lieutenant, I'm riding out now to hunt for Geronimo myself and I—"

"You?" Nelson interrupted. "Why?"

Sutton told him about Vernon Adams. "So as of the moment, Lieutenant, I'm on a cold trail. I figure if Geronimo can't tell me anything more about Adams, maybe one of his men might be able to."

"I asked you where he went. Do you know?"

"I know."

"Well, Mr. Sutton?"

"I'd rather not say. Were I to tell you it might turn out that you'd get to Geronimo first and maybe kill him and then where'd I be? With him shot dead? Along with his men maybe?"

"We don't intend to kill the Apaches. Not if we can help it."

"Maybe you'll find out that you can't help killing them. You might have to in order to save your own life and the lives of your troopers. No, Lieutenant, I'm not going to tell you where Geronimo went."

"I am not a stupid man, Sutton," Nelson began and Sutton noticed that he had dropped the "Mr." "When I questioned Chandler, I recall that he said he intended to warn Geronimo of our intent to return him to the reservation. It is an easy matter therefore to deduce that, like you, he knows where Geronimo was going. Since you won't tell me, I shall simply ask Chandler."

"You're welcome to do that, Lieutenant. But the way I see it, Chandler's got even less reason to tell you what he knows than I do. Especially after you ordering him locked up."

"The man looked to be half Apache himself," Nelson remarked and gave a disgusted grunt. "Those clothes he wears. The skin of his face is almost as dark as an Indian's. Were it not for his blond hair one could easily mistake him for an Apache. A half-blood at best."

With Nelson's contemptuous last sentence echoing in his mind, Sutton turned and went to his dun. As he swung into the saddle, he was aware of Nelson and Petry consulting together. He rode out of the camp and then urged the dun into a gallop, determined to put as much distance between himself and Nelson's company of troopers as he could and as fast as possible.

He had almost reached the north bank of the Gila River when he saw a man sprawled on the ground ahead of him, his horse standing nearby.

Cautiously, he rode toward the unmoving man who, when he reached him, groaned and sat up, shaking his head from side to side.

Sutton recognized the trooper who had been ordered to see to it that Chandler was jailed at the agency.

"What happened to you, trooper?" he asked as the man got shakily to his feet.

"Sir, my prisoner. He tricked me. He said his horse had thrown a shoe and couldn't walk. He got out of the saddle and so did I, and when I went up to him to have a look at his horse's foot—he got my sidearm away from me and he slugged me."

Sutton scanned the surrounding landscape. "Well, he's gone from around here and that's a fact."

"The lieutenant will skin me alive when I tell him," the trooper murmured, his eyes doleful. "Lieutenant Nelson doesn't hold much with what he calls 'unsoldierly behavior' and I guess me letting my prisoner get away from me will strike him as unsoldierly behavior."

"Nelson's green. He needs time to grow into his new job. It takes time for a man to ripen, same as grain. He'll do alright if you boys give him half a chance."

"Sir, he thinks the Army's nothing much more than a series of drills and duties done to the tune of the trumpeter's bugle. He can be hard on lowly privates like me."

"He'll find out there's more to soldiering than drills and stable call out here. If he catches up with Geronimo, he'll find that out real fast."

"I guess we all will, sir. Most of us troopers are about as green as the lieutenant is himself. Take me now. I've only been in one scrape with Apaches so far."

"I heard that you boys had some trouble with the Coyoteros up around Camp Apache."

"Yes, sir, we surely did. They're tricky fellows, those Apaches, and they don't fight at all the way we do."

Sutton nodded his agreement and then rode on toward the Gila River.

CHAPTER 8

As Sutton rode out of the river and in among the buildings of the agency, he heard himself hailed by Landell who was standing with Dr. Esmond not far away.

Sutton rode up to the men and Landell asked, "Would you by any chance know who or what lit the fire under Chandler? He rode through here not long ago, and I'd have to say he was riding as if Satan himself was chasing him."

"He didn't stop or even act as if he saw us," Esmond volunteered. "He just kept right on riding south."

"Lieutenant Nelson had him put under guard," Sutton stated. "Seems him and Chandler didn't see eye to eye on a number of matters. Nelson wanted Chandler put in whatever you've got around here that passes for a jail. I found the trooper over across the river, the one who was bringing Chandler in. Chandler got away from him and he's bound and determined to warn Geronimo."

Landell frowned. "Warn him about what?"

"Nelson's taking his troopers and going out to hunt for Geronimo and the men with him," Sutton said. "Chandler's taken it upon himself to let Geronimo know there'll soon be troopers following his trail."

Landell said, "I hope I never see that missionary again. A troublemaker born and bred if I ever saw one."

"Landell," Sutton said, "I'm in need of some stores and I'd appreciate it if you'd sell me some."

"Our provisions are kept over there," Landell said, pointing to a squat log building. "You'll probably find what you need there."

"Appreciate it." Moments later, Sutton entered the dim interior of the building, the walls of which were lined with well-stocked shelves. The floor was nearly covered with barrels and wooden crates.

Later, after paying the man in charge, he left with a supply of beans, salt pork, corn meal, canned tomatoes, and coffee and a Dutch oven.

He wrapped the items in his bedroll which he tied behind the cantle of his saddle with piggin' strings. The man from the store emerged and said, "Looks like you're planning to eat fairly well wherever it is you're going."

Sutton grinned. "I am. I've heard it said that a lean belly can't feed a fat brain."

Minutes later, the agency was behind him as he rode south through a valley where Gila woodpeckers were entering and leaving their nests in the tall branches of saguaros.

Days later, he rode between San Simon Creek on his left and the Pinaleno Mountains on his right. The sky above him was a golden glaze and the last of the sun's light glinted on the creek and gilded the peaks of the Pinalenos. Sutton found the already cooling air a welcome relief after the heat of the desert day.

When the sun vanished behind the Pinalenos, the sky above Sutton changed rapidly from gold to red and then as quickly to purple.

He turned the dun to the right and rode up into the foothills of the Pinalenos until he came to a small spring that bubbled out of a rock. There he dismounted, stripped the gear from his horse, and hung his saddle blanket over a branch of a scrub oak. A spiny lizard darted across his boots as he did so and disappeared in the chapparal.

He pulled some grass that had died in the shadows cast by the oak and used it to wipe his dun down. Then he led the animal to the spring and hobbled it there.

After gathering wood, he built a fire in a small circle of stones, unwrapped the provisions he had bought, and cut off a small square of salt pork which he used to grease his Dutch oven. He opened a can of tomatoes with his knife and ate them without bothering to heat them. He used the empty can to draw a little spring water into which he mixed some corn meal. When the mixture was the right consistency, he formed it into flat cakes which he placed inside the greased oven.

Then, after raking the coals of the fire with a branch from the oak tree until he had made a satisfactory bed of them, he placed the oven in the center of them where it rested on its three sturdy legs. He covered it with its heavy lid and then, scooping up some coals with a flat stone, he placed them evenly around the upturned lip of the oven's lid.

He rinsed the can in the spring, filled it with water and coffee grounds, and balanced it between two flat stones next to the oven.

Hunkering down, he waited for the coffee to boil, and when it did and most of the grounds had settled, he filled his cup and drank, idly watching the dun as it browsed in the chapparal growing lushly near the spring.

When the Indian bread biscuits were evenly done on both sides, he slid them out of the greased oven onto his tin plate and ate them one by one.

Wiping his fingers on the grass, he moved through the darkness to the spring where he washed his oven, plate, and cup.

After stamping out his fire, he spread his bedroll under an overhang not far from the spring where he had a good view of the valley below him and where, he knew, he would not be seen by anyone who might happen to be in the mountains above him.

He hunkered down and gazed out across the valley to where San Simon Creek, a moon-silvered ribbon flowed in the quiet night.

Where, he wondered. Geronimo. Chandler. Nelson and his troopers.

Would Chandler find Geronimo? Will I, he asked himself? Or will I just wind up wandering all over old Mexico finding nothing much more than ocelots and javelinas?

His thoughts of Geronimo both plaguing and pleasing him, Sutton was aware that the Apache leader might not be able to tell him anything more that would aid him in his hunt for Vernon Adams. But one of Geronimo's warriors might be able to, he reminded himself.

He looked up at the crescent moon and at the winking stars sprinkled around it. Then he stretched, yawned, and sat down on the rocky ground. He unstrapped his cartridge belt, placed his pistol by his side, pulled off his boots and hat, and lay down, wrapping his blanket around him.

Sleep ambushed him, bringing with it a dream in which he rode past a tree from which hung the lifeless bodies of more Apaches than he could count.

Sutton was surpised when he awoke to find the sun announcing that it was nearly high noon.

Must have been wearier than I thought, he mused as he got up, clapped his hat on his head, shook out his boots and pulled them on. He holstered his .44 and strapped the cartridge belt around his hips. Making his way to the spring, he knelt, scooped up water in both hands, and drank heartily.

He removed the hobbles from his dun and stood watching as the horse threw itself on the ground and, all four legs pointing straight at the sun, rolled about on its back, its lips drawn back as if in a grin, before getting to its feet again. As the animal went to the spring and dropped its head to drink, Sutton packed his gear and later saddled and bridled the dun.

He left it, reins trailing, and climbed up on the overhang. He stood there staring south, eyes narrowed against the sun's glare.

Dust.

Not much, he thought. But enough to make a man believe that at least one rider was raising it. Maybe more than one. Chandler maybe. Or Geronimo and his Apaches.

Or maybe, Sutton thought, some desert rat going who knows where. He turned and gazed northward. More dust. But this time he could see who was raising it because the wind was coming from the southeast and sending the clouds of dust billowing out behind and to the right of Nelson and his men.

And me, Sutton thought, I'm in the middle of that bunch of soldiers and whoever's heading for Mexico way up ahead of them. He leaped down from the overhang and a moment later he was mounted and heading down out of the foothills of the Pinalenos. He rode close to the ragged cover their outcroppings provided but he was uncomfortably aware that the sun was almost directly above him, its rays fully revealing his presence in the valley.

His stomach grumbled, but he put thoughts of breakfast out of his mind. He dug his heels into the flanks of the dun and went galloping through the tall needle grass that covered the floor of the valley and didn't ease up on the dun until he reached the spot where the grass was flattened directly beneath a soaring soap tree.

He circled the area. Noting the quantity of grass that was flattened, he decided that many men had slept here the night before. The only group who would be out here, he thought, are the Apaches I'm after. There's no settlements in the area. Nor even any ranches. And no animals that travel in herds—only wildcats and ringtail raccoons.

Sutton looked to the north. No sign of the troopers.

He rode at a right angle to the trail he had been following and, when he came to the creek, he dismounted and stood on its bank, staring down into the shallow water. A languid shadow beneath its surface caught his eye, moving slowly, seemingly aimlessly.

As his horse drank, Sutton knelt and pulled his knife from his boot as more shadows shifted beneath the water. He raised the knife, held it steady, waited. The shadows vanished.

Damn fool, he declared himself and then waded across the creek where he again knelt on its bank. My shadow spooked them. Again he waited, his knife poised.

Suddenly, it plunged into the water and when he raised his dripping hand, there was a squirming pupfish impaled on the knife's blade.

He scaled and gutted the fish, then sliced off its head and tail, and began to eat it raw, spitting out the bones. After he filled his canteen, he recrossed the creek and swung into the saddle.

He had finished eating the fish long before he came to the southernmost range of the Pinalenos. He rode with his eyes on the ground searching for sign of Apaches, aware that he had seen no sign of Chandler. None. Why, he wondered?

The next day, as he came within sight of the Chiricahua Mountains, he spotted the bones of a sidewinder lying white beneath the scorching sun. He slowed his dun and then halted it. As he did so, he spotted the snake's head lying some distance from the bones.

It's them, he thought happily. Geronimo and the others. Some one among them killed this rattler and ate it, skin and all. Whoever did it, tossed the head away after he'd cut it off so the critter's jaw wouldn't jerk shut in death and maybe close on his arm and kill him.

Sutton stood up in his stirrups but he could see nothing other than the land ahead of him out of which the Chiricahuas rose silent and faintly ominous. Well, he thought, at least Chandler told me the truth. It sure does look like Geronimo's heading down into Mexico because Arizona Territory ends not far beyond those mountains.

He rode on, sweat beading on his face and neck and running down to soak his shirt.

From time to time, he glanced over his shoulder but still he saw no sign of Nelson. Maybe he's given up the chase, he thought. Maybe he's willing to content himself with bringing a little law and order to the reservation. Maybe him and his men have turned back. Hope they have.

It was late afternoon when the mountains began to give way to low ridges and mounded foothills and Sutton, as he rode, saw the mountains of Mexico in the distance. Big place, Mexico, he thought. Big enough to hold whole tribesful of Apaches in the nooks and crannies of the two Sierra Madre ranges.

The sound of a horse's hooves clattering over loose rock somewhere behind him caused Sutton to turn the dun around and gallop back into a narrow and not very deep canyon between two of the foothills. He quickly dismounted and when his dun snorted, he clamped his left hand over its muzzle to quiet it. He listened. The sound of the hooves was closer now. A mustang? The dun tossed its head and he almost lost his grip on the animal's muzzle. Rider most likely. No mustang'd be wandering about out here in the desert.

And then the horse and rider galloped into view and Sutton immediately recognized Chandler aboard his black. They had come from the north and Sutton realized at once why he had not spotted any sign of Chandler earlier. *The man's been paralleling my course over on the western side of the Pinalenos and Chiricahuas.*

The sound of a bugle rang out, and the instant it did, Chandler looked back over his shoulder, tightened his grip on the reins, and slammed both moccasined feet into the black's ribs, causing the animal to bolt forward, its eyes wide, blood caused by the bite of the bit in its mouth dripping from its lips.

Sutton leaped aboard the dun and went galloping out of the canyon. He too heeled his horse in an effort to catch up with Chandler. When he did, he reached out, grabbed the black's bridle, and then, wheeling the dun in a tight circle, he galloped back the way he had come, holding tightly to the black's bridle.

"Luke!" Chandler yelled. "What—"

As both men rode over cracked sheets of shale the sound of their horses' hooves drowned out Chandler's words.

Sutton headed back into the canyon he had left moments ago. He drew rein and slid out of the saddle. He reached up, pulled Chandler down off the black, and then, running, led both horses deeper into the canyon. He wrapped both sets of reins around a prickly pear cactus, cutting his right hand on its thorns as he did so.

He loped back to where Chandler stood, grabbed the

missionary by the arm and hauled him up the sloping canyon wall. At its top, he pushed Chandler down to the ground and dropped beside him where both were sheltered by a thick growth of buckthorn.

Chandler, his breath coming in shallow gasps, tried to speak but couldn't.

"Save your breath to cool your coffee," Sutton muttered. "Look."

Both men stared down at the galloping troopers led by Lieutenant Nelson.

"My horse—" Chandler began, gasping. A moment later adding, "He was about done for. Those soldiers have been after me since—practically all afternoon."

"They've lost you. Look at them. They think you sprouted wings, you and your horse, and flew away."

Chandler laughed lightly as he watched Nelson call a halt, confer with Sergeant Petry, and then look to the right and left.

"I doubt those fellows know much about reading sign," Sutton said. "Even if they do, we rode over shale for a ways. They probably won't be able to trail us."

"They might reconnoiter the area," Chandler said, his breathing slower and deeper now. "They might find us."

"I don't reckon they will. Nelson might have wanted you but my bet's that he wants Geronimo more."

As Sutton and Chandler watched, Sergeant Petry rode back along the line of troopers, apparently giving them orders.

The line dissolved. Troopers dismounted. Some took charge of the horses. Two began to set up a rope corral.

"They're going to camp there tonight," Sutton said, an edge to his voice.

"Then we'll have to hole up here," Chandler said.

"For a spell. Come night, though, we can make our move."

"It seems I'm always in your debt, Luke."

"You don't owe me a damned thing, Chandler."

"Nelson would have caught me if you hadn't come along. My horse was about to drop under me. Neither one of us has had any water in over a day."

"We'll maybe find us some once we're on our way again. You'll just have to hold out till then."

Sutton watched as a trooper kindled a fire and he was still silently watching later as the men began to bed down for the night.

"Why did you do it?" Chandler asked him.

Sutton, his eyes on the sentry patrolling the sleeping camp, asked, "Do what?"

"Bring me here."

"Those soldiers might have shot you."

"Do you think they would have?"

"Don't know for certain. Do know, though, that they're a pretty green bunch. One or more of them might have got off a shot or two. This way, you'll have a better chance of catching up with your friends."

"How do you know they're green?"

"Talked to the one who was taking you to the agency. But, then, you can see the fact that they're green for yourself."

"I don't follow you, Luke."

"They built a fire. But they didn't do much cooking over it. They only have two pack mules with them."

"I'm still not sure what you're getting at."

"Looks to me like they didn't bring enough provisions with them. Only a green commander with men as green as himself would set out that way." Sutton slowly rose to his feet. "Time to try moving out."

Chandler also rose.

"I'm going down to get the horses. I'll bring them around to the mouth of the canyon. You climb down and meet me there."

Sutton, leading the dun and black several minutes later, left the canyon to find Chandler waiting for him. "We'll head east a ways to keep out of sight of that sentry."

As Chandler put a foot in the stirrup of his horse, Sutton said, "We'll walk, not ride. Less noisy that way."

Sutton set out, leading his dun, Chandler following him.

Before they had covered more than a few yards, a shriek shattered the stillness.

Sutton swung around, shoved Chandler out of his way so he could see the campfire, and then swore.

"What's going on back there?" Chandler asked, alarmed.

Figures ran in all directions, their legs silhouetted by the fire's flames. Shouts filled the darkness.

"Luke—"

"Your friends have come calling on Nelson and it's by no manner of means a social call." Sutton swung into the saddle and went galloping away from Chandler toward the troopers' camp.

With his .44 gripped tightly in his hand, he rode into the battle. His first shot unhorsed an Apache. As the horse went galloping away into the night, the man leaped to his feet, saw Sutton, and, with blood flowing from his left hand, lunged.

Sutton thrust out one booted foot. It caught the Apache just below his throat and sent him sprawling. Sutton fired a second time, killing the man.

Other shots sounded as troopers, bootless and wearing only their trousers, fired at their attackers.

When Sutton spotted Geronimo mounted on a sturdy

pinto, he rode toward the man, dropping another Apache as he went, the acrid odor of gunsmoke burning his nostrils.

As Geronimo raised a rifle and took aim at a trooper not far from him, Sutton seized the barrel of his rifle and yanked it from his hands.

"I've got shots left," he shouted at Geronimo over the noise of the battle. "One of them'll end your part in this little shindig." He didn't care whether or not Geronimo understood what he had said because he was certain that the man knew the danger he was in.

Geronimo, unarmed now, stared down at the .44 in Sutton's hand.

Sutton moved the dun forward, forcing it to nudge the pinto sideways. He pointed.

Geronimo turned and rode away, Sutton right behind him.

The shooting continued. So did the soldiers' shouts and the wordless whoops of the Apaches.

Sutton moved up until he was almost abreast of Geronimo. Releasing his hold on his reins, he reached out, intending to slap the rump of the pinto to speed its progress away from the embattled camp.

Chandler's voice behind Sutton ordered him to drop his gun.

"I just want to have a word with Geronimo," Sutton said evenly. "Then he's all yours if you still want him."

"Drop your gun, Luke," Chandler repeated.

Sutton dropped his .44.

Chandler spoke to Geronimo in his own language and then Geronimo shouted something at the top of his voice.

A moment later, the Apaches, most of them mounted but some of them on foot, fled the camp, Geronimo and Chandler bringing up the rear.

A trooper raised his carbine, aiming at Geronimo's back.

Sutton quickly picked up his gun and snapped off a shot that went tearing past the man, barely missing him, exactly as Sutton had intended.

Startled, the trooper lowered his carbine, turned, and, when he saw Sutton, cursed and raised the carbine again, aiming it this time at Sutton.

Nelson appeared at the trooper's side and barked an order.

The trooper lowered the carbine.

Sutton holstered his revolver and walked over to Nelson. "You lose any men?"

"I don't know," Nelson answered, looking around as if dazed. "It all happened so fast. Most of my men were asleep. Bates . . ." Nelson got down on one knee to examine a man who was lying at his feet. He reached out and placed a hand on the man's chest. He looked up at Sutton. "Bates—he's dead."

"You all right, Lieutenant?" Petry asked as he came running up to his commanding officer.

"I'm all right, Sergeant. Bates . . ." Nelson looked down at the dead man.

Petry glanced at Sutton who nodded grimly.

"Privates Albrecht and Riley are also dead, sir," Petry told Nelson.

Nelson slowly rose. "Any others?"

"Private Sloan's got a knife wound. Private McAlester was shot in the leg."

"They came out of nowhere," Nelson said softly. "One minute the night was empty and the next it wasn't."

"Your orders, sir?" Petry asked.

Nelson, gazing off into the distance, said nothing for a moment. And then, "We'll go after them, Sergeant."

"In the morning, sir?"

"Now!" Nelson thundered.

"Begging your pardon, sir. But we'll never find those redskins in the dark, sir."

"Sergeant Petry's right, Lieutenant," Sutton said. "You'll have a better chance of catching those Apaches in the daylight, though not the best chance on account of they're clever at concealing themselves."

"I'll appoint a burial detail, sir," Petry said. "See to the wounded men."

"Do that, Sergeant." Nelson turned his attention to Sutton. "You seem to know a thing or two about Apaches. You fought in the Indian wars?"

Sutton shook his head. "I scouted for the Army though. Got to be friends with a Lipan Apache. He taught me that thing or two you just mentioned."

"Friends? With an Apache?" Nelson's tone was incredulous.

"That's what I said, Lieutenant."

Nelson stared at him. Then he said, "I'm glad we caught up with you, Sutton. Your expertise will be most helpful to us in tracking down those red demons. Agent Landell told us he'd seen Chandler heading south so I reasoned that he must be heading the same way that Geronimo and his men had headed. However, our finding him, I must admit, was more good luck than good management. But with your help . . . We'll set out at first light."

Sutton said nothing.

First light found Sutton, after a few hours of shallow and fitful sleep and a surreptitious departure from the troopers' camp, riding a ragged trail through a forest of cardon cactus, the border of Arizona Territory behind him.

Ahead of him, judging by the sign he had seen, was Geronimo and his band—and Chandler.

Chandler, he thought. There's no doubt where the man's sympathies lie, not after he used his gun to make me drop mine before running off with his friends.

All I wanted to do was question Geronimo, he thought angrily. But maybe it looked to Chandler like I was about to throw down on him. Nope. That idea just won't hold water. I told Chandler I just wanted to ask a question or two. Well, the next time that Apache and me meet I'll ask my questions if I have to hog-tie Geronimo and run off his Apaches and Chandler right along with them.

He pulled his hat low on his forehead as the sun appeared in the east and rode out of the cardon cactus and down a rocky slope that was partially covered with grama grass and yellow paperflowers. His eyes roved the bowl of the valley before him. At first he saw nothing other than stretches of volcanic terrain to the south, thickly forested, and mountains on both sides blurred by early morning mist.

But then, just this side of the ridge on his left he saw something that was not rock, not shadow.

He saw a small building that was constructed of stone below a pole roof.

He walked the dun down the slope and then across land grooved by gullies which seemed to have erupted in places in low sharp ridges. His progress was slow because he had to ride to the right, then to the left, never able to move in a straight line toward his destination.

As he neared the building, he suddenly halted as an Apache came out of the stone structure followed by another one. A third emerged, dragging a young Mexican woman whose hair flew about her face as she clawed at her captor.

Geronimo appeared from behind the house and beckoned to the three Apaches. Sutton could tell that the four men were arguing. They gesticulated wildly, shaking their heads and their fists.

When the argument ended, the Apache holding the woman released her and she fled back toward the house.

Chandler appeared in the doorway.

The Apache who had held her captive raised his arm.

A knife, glinting, flew from his hand and buried itself high in the woman's back. She crumpled to the ground and then began to crawl crabwise along the ground toward Chandler whose legs suddenly buckled and began to give way. He went down on his knees and, as the band of Apaches mounted their ponies, his hands rose to cover his face and his shoulders hunched forward.

He was still in that position when Sutton, finally sure that the Apaches were gone, rode up to the building and wordlessly sat his saddle, staring down at the woman who no longer moved and at Chandler whose body trembled and whose tears slid between his fingers to streak his grimy hands.

Sutton looked to the south and was able to make out only the light haze of dust raised by the Apaches as they rode away.

Sutton looked back as Chandler began to babble incoherently. He watched Chandler's fingers drop down to reveal his wet cheeks and anguished eyes. He tried to make out what Chandler was saying.

"Chandler."

Chandler didn't look up at him. He got to his feet slowly, steadying himself by holding onto the door frame, still babbling but not as loudly, his voice now little more than a mutter.

"Chandler," Sutton said again and dismounted.

When Chandler didn't answer or seem to recognize him, he went up to the man, grasped him by both shoulders and shook him.

Chandler suddenly threw back his head and screamed, a high-pitched and agonized sound that caused Sutton's body to stiffen.

He released his hold on Chandler and stepped around him and into the building. The sight that met his eyes caused his teeth to grind together. He stood rigidly just inside the building, staring down.

A middle-aged Mexican woman lay on the dirt floor, her glazed eyes on the ceiling, bullet wounds in both of her breasts. In a shadowy corner not far away lay a man of about the same age as the dead woman, his skull crushed by the bloody stone crock that lay next to his body.

Sutton spun around as Chandler screamed, "I'll kill them! I will! Every one I can find! Slowly! I'll kill them *slowly!*"

Sutton went to the door and stepped outside. "Chandler, you'd best take it easy now. You'd best—"

Chandler pointed to the young dead woman just outside the door. "Do you know what they did to her? Before they killed her?" He began to sob. Moments later, he fell silent. With his back to Sutton, he said, "Her mother begged them not to. 'Take me instead,' she said. 'No one has ever touched my daughter.' They laughed at her. They *laughed!*"

Sutton reached out and got a grip on Chandler's shoulder.

"*No!* Don't you try to stop me!"

Sutton put out his other hand, reaching for Chandler's other shoulder, intending to turn the man around so he could speak to him, try to calm him.

Chandler spun around and his right fist shot out.

As Chandler's fist slammed into the side of his head, Sutton saw the world around him whirl and felt himself staggering.

Chandler hit him again with the same fist in the same place and Sutton went down and then down even deeper into an ebony ocean.

CHAPTER 9

Sutton, drowning in the deep ebony ocean, felt himself slowly ascend until he was sure he had entered hell's hot domain.

He struggled to escape, fought hard to be free . . . His eyes flicked open and then reflexively closed as the sun in the center of the sky blinded him where he lay on the ground beneath its relentlessly burning rays.

He groaned and sat up. Opening his eyes again, he saw his hat lying nearby and he reached out and picked it up. He put it on and then gingerly got to his feet, his skull throbbing. He swayed, caught his balance, and looked down at the body of the young woman the Apaches had murdered. He groaned again.

He went into the building and looked around. No shovel. Nothing at all to dig with. He went outside again and began to gather rocks.

More than an hour later, he placed the last rock on the last makeshift grave. He stood for a moment staring down at the three rocky mounds he had made and then abruptly turned away from them and walked toward his dun.

He halted as he caught sight of the troopers riding toward him, resigned to the fact that they had found him.

"I thought we had made an agreement," Nelson said testily as he drew rein beside Sutton. "You were to guide us to Geronimo."

"Lieutenant," Sutton said, "we didn't have any agreement. You went and decided for me what I was going to do next. But I didn't tell you I'd do it."

"I could order Sergeant Petry to put you under guard and force you to do what I asked."

"I reckon there's not much doubt that you could put me under guard, Lieutenant, but I'm not so sure that'd be enough to force me to point out sign to you. I could elect to just keep my mouth shut and let you and your boys wander all over this desert down here until you all wound up maybe damned but surely dead. What's more, I slipped away from you once and I reckon I can do the same again."

"My sentry discovered your absence from our camp during the night, Sutton," Nelson declared. "We set out after you immediately. We've been fortunate. We've found you. Now, I'm willing to admit that placing you under guard would not guarantee that you would perform the service I am asking of you. But surely you can see that we are both in this situation together and can be of help to one another. Please forget and forgive my mention of detention. Will you cooperate with us?"

Sutton was silent, considering the question, his eyes on Nelson's drawn face from which his haggard eyes burned. "I'll ride with you, Nelson. On one condition."

"One condition?"

"That if and when we catch up to those Apaches, you and your men will give me a free hand with Geronimo. You know I need to talk to him. So you ought to know, since you know that much, that I don't want him killed by some skittish trooper before I can talk to him."

"Agreed," Nelson said. "Sergeant Petry, make it known to the men that Sutton will be riding with us and the condition under which he has agreed to do so."

"Yes, sir," Petry responded. He turned his horse and rode back down the line of dusty troopers.

"How're you and your men fixed for water, Lieutenant?" Sutton inquired.

"Our supply is dangerously low."

"Detail some of your men to fill all your canteens from the river over there."

"That water's muddy," Nelson pointed out. "We checked it earlier."

"You!" Sutton said, pointing at the young trooper who had earlier been assigned to guard Chandler. "What's your name?"

"Carter, sir."

"Carter, you gather up the canteens and take them down to the river."

"Sir," Carter began hesitantly, "that river water's thick with silt."

"Just listen, Carter," Sutton said. "Dig an Indian well—that's a deep hole ten, fifteen feet from the bank. It'll start filling up with water—muddy water. Bail it out and keep bailing and pretty soon clear water'll start to fill the hole. Then fill the canteens."

Carter glanced uneasily at Nelson.

"Do as he says, trooper," Nelson ordered and Carter began to collect the men's canteens.

"Nelson, it looks to me like you're low on provisions too judging by the small size of the packs those two mules of yours are carrying."

"Lamentably so," Nelson admitted.

"Have somebody scavenge about inside that house to see what they can come up with."

"Steal?" Nelson's expression was one of shock.

Sutton pointed to the three graves. "Apaches killed the people who lived here not long before you rode up. Any provisions inside that house won't do those people any good and they will do us some good."

"But that amounts to robbing the dead," Nelson protested.

"Reckon it does. You figure they'd mind?"

Nelson hesitated and then gave the order to search the house. He got out of the saddle and said, "Sutton, do you have any more orders to give my men? Or me?"

Sutton caught the sardonic edge to Nelson's voice. "Lieutenant, I'm just trying to be helpful. If I've gone and set your teeth to grinding together—"

Nelson held up a hand. "Please overlook my testiness, Sutton. It's been a long hot ride through unfamiliar territory and I'm easily as tired as most of my men are. However, I realize that fact is no excuse for discourtesy or pique. I hope you'll overlook my—"

"Might be a good idea to see to the horses before we set out," Sutton interrupted.

Nelson gave the order and the troopers proceeded to carry it out. "Where do you think they've gone?"

"The Apaches?" Sutton stroked his stubbled chin. "South, that much is for certain. Where exactly—well, I'll venture a guess. Deep into the desert where they might figure we won't follow them."

"But we will!" Nelson said, his voice low, sounding as if he were assuring himself that he would continue the pursuit.

"Nothing much down south of here but sand and sun. That won't bother an Apache any more than a mosquito or two would, but I expect it'll be hard on you and your men."

"We're soldiers, Sutton!"

Sutton nodded. "Soldiers sweat as much as the next man. Thirst as easy too."

"The canteens are being filled," Nelson reminded Sutton.

"Sir," said a trooper who wore the chevrons of a saddler, "we found some flour and beans in the house."

"Good," Nelson said. "Pack them."

"Get some men to help you take the horses down to the river, Corporal," Sutton said as the trooper was about to turn away. "Water them well."

An hour later, Nelson gave the order to move out.

Sutton countermanded it.

When Nelson, holding his evident anger in check, asked for an explanation, Sutton replied, "The horses need to be fed. The men too. All of them could use some rest judging by the looks of them."

Nelson gave an order and the trooper who wore a yellow chevron with a baker's hat above it began to build a fire.

Sutton unpacked his skillet and provisions and gave them to the man.

Two hours later, Nelson moved his men out, Sergeant Petry riding on his right, Sutton on his left.

They rode in a silence that was broken only by the jingling of harness and the sound of horseshoes striking stone. Sutton alternately scanned the ground over which they rode and the surrounding countryside.

The sloping land gave way to a relatively flat vista that was broken only by an occasional barrel cactus. Sutton, when he spotted horse droppings, pointed them out to Nelson.

"Apaches?" Nelson asked.

"Those droppings are all dried out," Sutton observed. "That don't tell us much though about how long ago the Apaches—if it was them—passed this way considering how hot the sun is. It's damned near hot enough to have dried those droppings before they even hit the ground."

Nelson managed a wan smile.

They rode on over the sandy wasteland as a few clouds materialized in the sky above them, none of which ever came near enough to the sun to hide it and offer them a respite, however brief, from the heat.

"We'd best stop for a spell," Sutton said. "Have the men break out their tarps, blankets, or tents if they have any for some kind of cover. We'll move on once the sun's down."

Nelson called a halt and Petry relayed Sutton's suggestion in the form of an order to the troopers who began to rig whatever kind of shelter they could manage.

"You're right welcome, sir, to share my lean-to," Private Carter said to Sutton and indicated the shelter he had constructed.

"Much obliged." Sutton, using his hat, watered his dun and then entered the lean-to Carter had made out of a blanket. He sat down beneath it, Carter, his knees up and his forearms resting on them, beside him.

"It gets hot in Georgia," Carter said, "but not ever like it does out here. This here's a land to wring a man bone dry."

"That where you're from, Carter? Georgia?"

"Yes, sir. Near Stone Mountain outside of Atlanta. I can tell you I wouldn't mind to find myself sitting in the shade of that old mountain right this very minute."

"You been soldiering long?"

"Not long. Be a year come August."

"How's it agreeing with you, soldiering?"

"To tell you the truth, sir, it's not near to what I had it figured for. I thought it would be—well, flags and trumpets and spit and polish and pretty girls standing by giving me looks fit to send shivers up my spine. What it's turned out to be mostly, though, is dirt and more dirt and being always on the go so that a man has trouble remembering in the morning where he was the night before. And girls —I haven't seen a single one that wasn't already took by some officer or other. No, soldiering, it's not like it is in the stories I used to read when I was young."

Sutton suppressed a smile. "How old are you?"

"Nineteen." Carter picked up his canteen, opened it, and began to drink.

Sutton reached out and took it away from him, causing Carter to splutter his surprise at Sutton's unexpected action. "Take it easy on that water. You don't know how long it's going to have to last you. What's more, there's your horse to consider. I'd suggest you plan on giving him twice as much each day as you give yourself and that you give yourself as little as possible. A swallow every hour ought to be about right."

"I could empty this canteen right this very minute, I'm that parched."

Sutton handed it back.

"You reckon we'll find those Indians we're chasing, sir?"

"We might. There's a chance we will."

"They're not likely to let us take them without putting up something of a fight, are they?"

"They'll fight all right."

"You ever fought Apaches before?"

"When I was with the Army, I did, a time or two."

"They don't fight like decent men. They're dirty fighters, those Apaches."

"They fight any way they think will let them win, and that's what fighting's all about when you come right down to it."

Carter glanced at Sutton who was staring out at the

desert. "I guess maybe you're right. Sometimes, when I think about what's happening to them—you know, the way they're being rounded up and put on reservations and told to do this and not to do that—if a bunch of soldiers or Indians or anybody had ever tried to do that to us old boys back in Georgia, why, we'd have had our shotguns out up there in the hills and we'd fight too, we would, and maybe we wouldn't fight in ways you could call fair neither."

"I see you've got my point." Sutton's eyes narrowed.

Carter, watching him, looked out at the desert. And then back at Sutton. "You see something, sir?"

"Sand's shifting. See there? See those little funnels of sand lifting up into the air?"

"I see them. I thought maybe you'd spotted Apaches."

"I may have spotted something almost as bad."

"Sir?"

"Wind's rising. Rising fast. We could be about to have ourselves a sandstorm."

"Well, I don't think I could get much dirtier than I already am. I reckon I can stand a little sand next to my skin if it don't turn out to itch too bad."

Sutton left the lean-to and looked up at the cobalt sky from which the white clouds were being swept by the wind. He turned and then turned again until he had established the fact that the wind was coming from the west. It swept down out of the western range of the Sierra Madres, already blurred by the sand being lifted into the air by the steadily and swiftly rising currents.

"This sand sure stings," Carter commented as he appeared beside Sutton.

Sutton, blinking and turning away from the wind, reached for his horse's reins and began to walk, shoulders

hunched and hat pulled down low on his forehead, to the
east.

"Where you headed, sir?" Carter called out to him.

Sutton merely pointed to the barrel cactus that was his
destination. He was aware of troopers scurrying about on
both sides of him and of horses snorting their uneasiness as
the sand struck and abraded their hides.

He stumbled as the sand seemed to fly out from beneath
his boots. Regaining his balance, he plodded on under the
sky which was now almost invisible above him, the sun in
it a pale disk that gave little light and less heat, being
partially obscured by the blowing sand in the hot dry air.

A horse bolted past him. It fell, struggled to its feet, and
ran on.

A trooper ran past him, cursing.

Sutton recognized Carter. "Let him go!" he shouted.
"Take cover!"

But Carter ran on as Sutton's shouts were whirled away
by the wind. A moment later, he and the horse he was
pursuing both disappeared in the blowing sand.

Sutton reached the barrel cactus and took up a position
downwind of it. He removed his bandanna and tied it
around the dun's eyes. Then he threw the horse which,
because of the blindfold, lay quietly on its right side near
the base of the cactus.

He sat down and braced his back against the horse's
belly, running a soothing hand down first one of the animal's forelegs and then the other. Between barely parted
lips he spoke softly to the dun in an effort to keep it quiet.

Sand buffeted his back and stung his neck. He turned
up the collar of his shirt and then untied his bedroll. He
draped his blanket over his head and around his shoulders, making his body a small ball as he huddled against

his horse and the sand continued to fly and the wind to whine over his head.

He could hear men shouting in the distance but he could not make out their words. Their voices were at times far away and then closer before they faded away into the wind again.

As time passed and Sutton sheltered beneath his blanket, the voices died away completely and the world held only the keening wind and the blowing sand. His body involuntarily slid away from his horse as the wind whipped the sand away on one side of him to leave a deep basin into which he slipped. His blanket fell free. He grabbed it and, keeping his mouth tightly shut and holding his breath in order to avoid inhaling sand, wrapped it around himself again and crawled back to his living windbreak, the dun.

More time passed and still the wind tore across the desert's dunes to send them shifting and sliding into new shapes. Not long afterward these too were altered by the relentless wind, which shrieked in Sutton's ears as the sand drifted up against his body, almost burying it at one point and making him alter his position.

He heard a horse nicker nearby and he pressed his body as close to the dun as he could. When he felt the animal's body lurch, he threw off his blanket just in time to see one of the trooper's mounts which was about to step on his dun a second time. He let out a yell and flapped his blanket in the face of the horse, which shied and then turned and raced away.

He changed position once more so that he could cover the dun's muzzle with his own arched body to keep the horse from choking on the sand that was swirling around the animal. He remained in that position for an unmeasurable amount of time, his muscles stiffening and beginning to ache. But he did not move—except for his left hand which gently stroked the horse's neck and his lips from which came wordless sounds as he sought to soothe the animal.

He could feel the sand piling up against his body and covering his legs. Still he did not move.

The wind did, however, roaming across the desert and lashing the barren landscape. The sand did too, as it was picked up and hurled high into the sky.

The dun stirred.

Sutton continued stroking it and whispering to it.

The animal quieted.

So, hours later, did the wind. Slowly at first and then more rapidly it diminished and finally died away altogether.

Sutton pulled his legs free of the sand that had buried them and pulled off his blanket. He untied the dun's blindfold and stood up at the same time that the horse did.

He looked up at the sky placid with its nightly tenants, the crescent moon and the stars. He wrapped the reins of his dun around his right wrist and then sat down and pulled off his boots. He shook the sand from them before putting them back on again.

He hobbled the dun and removed his gear from it, shaking the sand from his saddle blanket and saddlebags.

Around him the desert was cool, the air fresh and vibrant with the scent of saguaro blossoms despite the fact that many of them, vividly white in the moon's silent light, had been torn and shredded by the wind-whipped sand.

In the distance, men and horses were moving.

Sutton, his boots sinking in the sand, walked over to a pair of men and two horses, aware that the desert had taken on a new shape and structure during the storm as if it had been reborn, a birth wrought by the wind.

"I feel like I've been rawhided," one of the troopers, his mustache thick with sand, was saying as Sutton came up to him.

"That was some sonofabitching storm!" grumbled the other trooper.

"Where's Lieutenant Nelson?" Sutton asked.

Both troopers looked around, shrugged.

"My throat's dry as dust," one of them said. "I'm going to empty my canteen in one big long swallow." He turned toward the horse that was standing behind him. "Hey, this isn't my mount." He turned toward the other horse. "Neither's this one."

"That one's mine," the other trooper said. "I don't know who belongs to this other one."

"Well, I'm going to hunt mine down," the first trooper said. "Neither one of these two has a canteen."

Sutton's eyes darted from one horse to the other. It was true, he realized. No canteens hung from the saddle horns of either animal.

He walked as quickly as he could over the low dunes to where another horse stood alone, its eyes tearing. He examined it and found that it too carried no canteen.

"Sutton!"

He turned to find Nelson coming toward him, leading his horse and accompanied by several troopers on foot.

"Lieutenant," Sutton said as Nelson reached him, "where's your canteen?"

Nelson looked over his shoulder. "It's—why, it's gone!"

"So are some of our horses, sir," said one of the troopers with Nelson.

"We had trouble with the horses when the storm struck," Nelson told Sutton. "I finally ordered the men to look out for their own protection. My canteen must have been blown loose by the wind. Corporal Mellon, search for it."

"You won't find it, Mellon," Sutton said quietly.

"You think it's been covered by sand, Sutton?" Nelson asked.

"I think it's been taken, along with most of the other men's canteens—maybe all of them."

"Taken?" Nelson frowned.

"By Apaches."

"I saw no Apaches," Nelson declared. "You men—did you see any Indians during the storm?"

"No, sir," Mellon answered. "The whole bunch of us were holed up together under our tarps and blankets the whole time."

"They came in under cover of the storm," Sutton said. "Stole your water."

"That makes no sense!" Nelson spluttered. "They could have killed us had they done that and obviously we're still alive."

"Some Apaches have a twisted sense of humor, Lieutenant," Sutton remarked. "Some of them take a perverse pleasure in watching their enemies die slow—of thirst maybe."

"We'll find a stream," Nelson stated confidently. "An oasis perhaps."

"We might, but meanwhile you and your men and your mounts'll have a hard time without water. Bearing that fact in mind, it's my suggestion that we move out right now. By midmorning, we'll have to take cover again on account of the sun."

"I have to have a head count," Nelson said, "and my men have to search for their strayed horses."

"Well, your men had best be quick about their counting and their hunting, Lieutenant."

But the troopers were not. It was an hour before dawn when Nelson received the report, in Sutton's presence, that five of the horses had been lost along with Private Carter.

"No sign of any of them," concluded Corporal Mellon who had reported the bad news to Nelson.

"They wandered off," Nelson mused. "They became lost in the storm."

"Or they were took by the Apaches."

The eyes of the lieutenant and corporal turned accusingly on Sutton as if he had just insulted them.

"I'm not claiming that's what happened," he said. "I'm just saying that's what might have happened."

"Have the men get ready to move out," Nelson shouted to Sergeant Petry who was standing nearby with a handkerchief, trying to wipe away the sand that was crusted around his mount's eyes.

Within the hour they moved out, an unmilitary column of apprehensive troopers, with Sutton again riding on the left of Lieutenant Nelson. Sutton was well aware that Nelson was doing his best to look composed, even confident, as he sat straight in the saddle, seemingly unmindful of the early morning but already hot sun.

Sutton rode and sweated, sweated and rode. "Lieutenant," he said some time later, "head your men over that way." He pointed.

"Why?"

"There's pigweed growing this side of those low buttes. See it?"

"I see the rocks but—"

"Follow me." Sutton cut in front of Nelson and Petry and rode at right angles to their former line of march, heading for the buttes he had pointed out. Behind him, he heard Petry order the column to make a right turn. When he reached his destination, he got out of the saddle, and hunkered down to wait.

When the troopers reached him, he looked up at Nelson and said, "This here's pigweed." He pointed to the plants growing in clusters about his boots which were about eight inches tall with reddish-green leaves and stems. "Have your men harvest these. They can keep them in their saddlebags."

"To what purpose, Sutton?"

Instead of answering Nelson directly, Sutton plucked one of the plants and began to chew its stem. He plucked another one and handed it up to Nelson who, imitating Sutton, began to chew the plant's stem.

"Why, it contains quite a bit of water!" he exclaimed a moment later. His face flushed with pleasure. "Sergeant, have the men do as Sutton has suggested."

When the plants had been torn from the ground and stored in the troopers' saddlebags, the column moved out again.

This time they had gone only a short distance when Sutton suddenly held up a hand and Petry promptly brought the troopers to a halt.

"What is it, Sutton?" the sergeant asked nervously. "Have you seen something?"

"I spotted something. Up ahead of us. A man, looks like."

"I don't see anybody," Petry remarked, shielding his eyes from the sun as he squinted into the distance.

"On the ground," Sutton told him. "He looks a lot like just another shadow."

"I see him."

"Is it Carter?" Nelson asked uneasily.

"Can't tell, sir," Petry replied. "Shall we investigate?"

Sutton didn't hear Nelson's answer to Petry's question because he was riding toward the figure sprawled on the sand. When he reached the man, his hand went to the butt of his revolver as he sat his saddle staring down at the Apache who lay on his back, his eyes closed.

The blood from the bullet wound in his throat no longer flowed.

Dead, Sutton thought and then was surprised to see the man stir feebly. He slid out of the saddle and got down on one knee beside the Apache who was obviously dying. He gripped the man's shoulder and squeezed. When the Apache's eyes opened to mere slits, Sutton quickly signed a question.

The Apache tried to speak but only guttural sounds emerged from his mouth and his efforts caused blood to begin to seep again from his wound. He raised both hands inches from the ground and answered Sutton's question in clumsy sign language as the troopers rode up.

But Sutton had understood although the movements of the Apache's hands had not formed the signs clearly.

White dog.

The Apache's answer could mean that Private Carter had shot the Indian. But there was another possibility, Sutton thought. Chandler. Might be maybe it was Chandler killed him. That missionary sure went loco back there at that Mexican adobe—a man crazed for revenge.

"What happened to that Indian?" Nelson asked, coming forward.

"Somebody shot him," Sutton replied and straightened up. He used his hands to talk to the Apache again and the dying man made brief responses in sign language.

"What's going on, Sutton?" Nelson asked testily.

"We're having us a powwow, him and me. But I'm not

finding out what I want to know from him, which is where we can find Geronimo and his boys. All he'll say is that they'll kill the white dog who killed him—and all of us too if we keep after them."

Sutton watched the Apache's eyes slide shut. "He's dead. Let's ride."

Less than an hour later, they saw the Indians ranged in a long line along a ridge of the western Sierra Madres, Geronimo among them.

"There they are, sir!" Petry cried and gave a whoop of delight. "Let's go get 'em! Sir?"

"Forward, ho!" Nelson shouted, his right arm raised, began to gallop toward the skylined Indians.

"Hold *on!*" Sutton yelled at him, exasperated.

Nelson drew rein and threw a look over his shoulder at Sutton.

Sutton rode up to him. "Those Apaches'd kill you all before you got halfway up the mountain. Besides, they're not letting you see them just for the fun of it. They got themselves a purpose. If you look real sharp into the shadows thrown down by the mountains, you'll see what their purpose is."

Nelson stared at the shadowy ground in front of the mountain range. So did Petry.

"Man coming this way," Sutton told them.

"A white man, sir!" Petry cried as the naked figure emerged from the shadows and came staggering across the desert toward them, one arm raised in a weak greeting, the other clutching his groin.

"Private Carter," Sutton said solemnly as the man fell, rose, and then staggered on, his sunburned body streaked with sand and blood.

"Good Lord!" Nelson breathed as Carter came closer. "Oh, good Lord, what have they done to the boy?"

Sutton said nothing as Carter fell again. Got up. Came on.

"His eyes, sir," Petry muttered, his hand tightening on his reins. "His—"

Carter had almost reached them when he collapsed and lay in a crumpled tangle of twisted limbs on the desert floor. His moans reached the men watching him.

Sutton heeled his horse and galloped up to Carter. He got out of the saddle, knelt down, and turned the trooper over to gaze into Carter's agonized eyes from which the eyelids had been cut away. He looked down at the boy's grossly mutilated body and then up as Nelson and the others arrived beside him.

He looked down again as Carter spoke, his voice a mumble. He bent down closer as Carter spoke again and tried to smile.

"No, boy," Sutton said soberly, "you're right. The Army's not all bugles and banners."

"—hell."

Sutton wasn't sure whether Carter's single word was meant to describe the Army or whether he had merely sworn. He shifted position so the shadow of his body fell across the face and body of Carter, shielding him, particularly his lidless eyes, from the sun.

He was still sitting there on the sand a short time later, Carter's head resting in his lap, when Carter died.

"Loss of blood," he told Nelson, who stood, his face forlorn, beside him. Then he looked up at the ridge.

The Apaches had disappeared.

"Sending Carter back here, Lieutenant," he said, "was meant as a warning. They maybe took him when they snuck up on us during the sandstorm. Or maybe they found him wandering around lost in it. Don't matter much now which way it really was."

"Warn me, will they?" Nelson snapped angrily, his fists clenched at his sides. "It is presumptuous of those savages to assume that I would accept their warning which, I assure you, Sutton, I will *not!* I will see every last one of those murdering, mutilating bastards dead first if I have to kill them all with my bare hands!"

"Lieutenant, we got us a bargain, you and me. So if it's killing you've got on your mind, you'd do well to remember that bargain of ours. If you so much as lift a little finger to harm Geronimo, you'll have me to deal with 'cause he's just about my last link to Vernon Adams and I'm bound and determined to talk to him about that matter."

Nelson met Sutton's steady gaze and then his lips slowly parted in an ugly snarl.

CHAPTER 10

White dog.

Chandler? Or Carter? Sutton suspected that it was Chandler who had killed the Apache back along the trail. But he knew there was an outside chance that it could have been Carter, although he doubted it. Carter had been the Apaches' prisoner and it wasn't likely that they'd have given him a chance to kill one of their own while they had him in custody.

Chandler. The man's a mystery, Sutton thought. He's the first missionary I ever have met who went about killing Indians. Indians he claimed were his close, if not closest, friends to boot. And all because he saw what they did to that Mexican family. Well, it sure wasn't a pretty sight. It was a sight that might help to unhinge a man. But, Sutton thought, Chandler must have known that the Apaches had been pillaging and slaughtering for years, both in Mexico and in the Territory up north—practically all over the Southwest in fact. But knowing it's happened and seeing it done's two different things. Hearing tales told about bloodshed's a whole lot different than seeing bodies bleeding right in front of your own two eyes.

Sutton's thoughts were shattered by the sound of a shot. He drew rein, staring up at the ragged peaks of the mountain range in front of him, and then realized that the shot had not been aimed at them. It had been fired in the mountains but not at the approaching column of cavalry.

Nelson gave a command and the troopers, most mounted but some on foot because they had lost their horses during the sandstorm, moved at a gallop and a run toward the foothills. They quickly took cover, certain troopers holding four mounts apiece as the others formed a thin skirmish line.

Sutton slid out of the saddle and quickly led his dun to the shelter of a small hill. He left it there in charge of one of the troopers who was holding other horses. He pulled his Winchester from its scabbard and, crouching low, made his way back to the skirmish line. He dropped down on the ground beside Sergeant Petry.

A shot went over his head and he fired at the spot where a puff of gunsmoke was faintly visible high above him.

His fire was promptly returned and then gunfire off to his left caused him to shift position. When an Apache's head rose above a ledge, he brought his carbine up and was about to fire when, to his surprise, the Indian rose, dropped his gun and pitched forward onto the rocks far below the ledge.

"What do you make of that?" Petry asked him. "None of us were firing at that savage. None of us ever even saw him."

Sutton had no time to answer the sergeant's question because the skirmish line took a volley of shots from the invisible Apaches in the mountains above them. The troopers and Sutton returned the fire, their targets not bodies but the gunsmoke that betrayed the presence of the hidden Apaches.

Then a single shot rang out and a trooper screamed, dropped his gun, and fell backward, a small red hole blossoming in his right cheek.

As the trooper thrashed about on the ground, still screaming, Sutton fired at the spot where the shot had come from. Although he had fired blindly with little hope of hitting his unseen target, an Apache suddenly bolted from a crevice, his weapon nowhere in sight, his hands frantically reaching behind him.

Sutton kept his eyes on the man. He saw him fall but knew he hadn't hit him. It was evident that the man had been shot in the back by someone Sutton could not see.

White dog.

The two words resounded in Sutton's mind and he thought, *Chandler.* He's up there somewhere and bent on killing himself some Apaches or I miss my guess. Bent on finishing what he started with that first dead Indian back along the trail.

"Howitzers," Petry muttered from his position next to Sutton as he squinted up into the mountains. "We should have at least one howitzer with us. We could blast half the mountain down with a few well-placed twelve-pound shells and some cannisters of shot."

"But all you've got, Sergeant," Sutton said, "is a bunch of green boys and many of them without mounts which turns them into infantrymen, not cavalry troopers."

"Look!" Petry said and fired at an Apache who had stepped out from behind a tree and was taking aim at the skirmish line. "Missed the damned devil!" Petry quickly reloaded but the Apache had vanished.

"Sergeant!" Nelson called from the rear.

"Sir?"

"Move a third of the men up into the mountains. Order them to engage the Indians—chase them down from the mountain. We'll meet them with a cavalry charge as they come down."

Petry barked a command and then another.

Some of the troopers rose hesitantly and then bolted

forward, dodging among the rocks and occasional junipers, firing as they ran.

Sutton scrambled along the ground to his left and when he had reached a stand of dead scrub oak, he ran in among the trees. Racing on, he suddenly swerved and began to climb the mountain, the sound of gunfire behind him urging him on as he climbed higher and higher until he was above the Apaches' battle line.

From where he crouched on a slab of rimrock, he could look down on a pair of Apaches who were firing, reloading, and then firing again at the figures of the skirmishers as they darted from cover to cover in their slow ascent.

Farther below him, he could make out Nelson and the remaining troopers mounting their horses.

They're likely as not to charge their own men, he thought, annoyance with Nelson bitter within him. But then, as he watched, Nelson led his men up the hill, their boots straining against their stirrups, the manes of their mounts flying.

His annoyance turned to awe and then to admiration as he watched Nelson and the men weave skillfully in and out among the skirmishers who then raced after the mounted and charging troopers.

An Apache yell split the air like the sound of glass shattering and the Indian who had uttered it threw a tomahawk at the advancing men.

The weapon split the skull of a trooper who went down without making a sound.

To the right and above the exultantly whooping Apache, a figure rose, aimed an Army Colt at him, and fired.

There's the white dog, Sutton thought, as the Apache fell and lay face down at the base of a piñon.

"Chandler!" Sutton yelled at the top of his voice, knowing that he was revealing his position but determined to stop the man from possibly killing Geronimo.

Chandler, momentarily startled, glanced in Sutton's direction and then away as he took aim again at another Apache below him.

Sutton wondered if his shouting of Chandler's name had alerted the Indian to the danger he was in because the man turned, saw Chandler above him, and snapped off a shot.

Chandler spun around, wounded in the left arm, and dropped down out of sight.

Sutton was up and running over the rimrock. He leaped across a crevice, climbed up to a higher level of rocky ground, and then ran along it to where he had last seen Chandler. But when he reached the spot Chandler was gone.

Or have I come to the wrong spot? Sutton asked himself. No, this was where he was. I recognize that rocky wall from the iron pyrites in it. He was standing right in front of it.

Yells from below caused him to spin around and look down.

Nelson and his men, both those astride horses and those on foot, were engaged in a bloody battle at close quarters with the Apaches.

Sutton took quick aim and fired, downing an Apache who had pulled a trooper out of the saddle and was about to gut the man with a gleaming scalping knife. Then he turned back and searched the area, looking for sign of Chandler but finding none. Not at first. Then a broken branch low on an oak caught his eye. The tree was some distance below him and he started down toward it, sliding as he made his descent and struggling to keep from falling headlong.

The rifle fire from below continued. So did the shouts and curses of the battling men.

Sutton looked around, stepped back—and suddenly slipped. He slid down the side of the mountain and almost went over the top of a cliff above a draw but he was able to stop his slide by grabbing with his left arm the trunk of a young pine. For a moment, he hung, his legs dangling over the edge of the draw, unwilling to move, fearing that if he did move he might dislodge the pine which he suspected had no deep roots in the shallow soil where it had sprouted as a seed.

He did move when he heard the shrill voice begin to scream below him. He gingerly eased his legs up under him and, still gripping the trunk of the tree, moved backward, listening.

Sutton got to his knees, leaned over, and peered down into the draw at Chandler and Geronimo. Chandler, with his back to Sutton and the sun, stood, his wounded left arm hanging bloody and useless at his side, pointing his revolver at Geronimo who stood facing him, arms folded across his chest, broad face impassive, black eyes glinting.

"Murderers!" Chandler screamed.

Sutton heard the anguished sobs that suddenly caused Chandler's body to convulse and his gun hand to waver. Sutton got to his feet and shouted a challenge. "You kill Geronimo and I'll kill you, Chandler!"

Chandler's head whipped around and he blinked up at Sutton silhouetted against the sun. He shifted position slightly so that his gun remained trained on Geronimo who had not moved nor spoken.

"I'm going to kill him the same way I killed that Apache back on the trail and those others here in the mountains for what they did." Chandler's voice, as he accepted Sutton's challenge, had been low, almost inaudible.

Sutton's finger tightened on the trigger of his Winchester. He didn't want to kill Chandler but he knew he would if the missionary made any attempt to kill Geronimo.

"You should be helping me kill these savages," Chandler suddenly yelled up to Sutton, "not trying to stop me."

Sutton recognized the counterchallenge behind Chandler's words. He raised his Winchester and sighted along its barrel.

Geronimo chose that moment to reach out and deftly wrest Chandler's revolver from the man's hand.

As Geronimo stepped back and cocked the revolver, his face animated now and his lips slightly parted, Sutton leaped from the rimrock and landed heavily on Chandler, taking the man down to the ground with him.

The force of his fall knocked Sutton's rifle from his hand and, as he reached out to retrieve it, he lost his grip on Chandler who took the opportunity to squirm out from under him and scramble to his feet.

Sutton seized his rifle with his left hand and with his right made a grab for Chandler's ankle. As his fingers closed around it, he jerked hard and Chandler went down, the breath gusting from his lungs.

Geronimo, standing some distance away, fired at Chandler, but Sutton, having seen out of the corner of his eye what the Apache was about to do, shoved Chandler out of the bullet's path.

Before Geronimo could fire again, Sutton, still down on the ground, brought his Winchester up and leveled it at Geronimo's midsection.

Geronimo grunted, his eyes on the rifle in Sutton's hand.

"Drop it," Sutton ordered him. "Chandler, tell him in Apache what I said."

Chandler, on his hands and knees, spoke to Geronimo

and Geronimo, without taking his eyes from Sutton's face, let Chandler's revolver fall from his hand.

Chandler crawled quickly along the ground and reached out for the weapon. But Sutton moved faster. He sprang to his feet and kicked the gun out of Chandler's reach.

Chandler uttered a wordless roar as he rose to his feet and, crouching with his fisted right hand raised, confronted Sutton. "He killed them," he said, his breathing shallow, his eyes glaring at Sutton. "I'm going to kill him and every other Apache I can get close to if it takes me my lifetime!"

"Chandler, use your head. I can understand that you're upset by what you saw happen to those Mexicans but pouring blood on blood won't solve a thing nor will it let you rest easy in the end."

"I'm not talking about *Mexicans!*"

"You're not?" Sutton stared at Chandler, puzzled, his forehead furrowed.

Chandler opened his mouth to speak but his words were drowned out by the sound of men and horses climbing the mountain behind Sutton.

Sutton turned to find Nelson and Sergeant Petry, accompanied by two troopers, entering the draw. "How'd you and your men make out, Lieutenant?" he inquired as Nelson rode up to him and drew rein.

"Four dead," Nelson responded curtly.

"Seven wounded," Petry added as curtly.

"The Apaches?"

Sutton saw Nelson's stony gaze flick toward Geronimo and remain on the leader's face.

After a moment had passed, Nelson looked back at Sutton and answered, "Most of them are dead. A few fled. We'll find them. The rest we're holding as prisoners down below. They will be returned to the reservation. So will he be." Nelson pointed a stiff finger at Geronimo.

"No!" Chandler shouted and dived for his revolver that was lying on the ground.

Sutton lunged forward. He seized a fistful of Chandler's loose tunic and jerked the man backward before he could get his hands on his gun. He marched Chandler over to Nelson and said, "You'd best keep an eye on him. He's been killing Apaches and he's hell-bent on killing Geronimo. Aren't you, Chandler?"

"Stop calling me that!"

"Stop calling you what?"

"Chandler."

Sutton, mystified, could only stare at the man who was now facing him.

"My name is Vernon Adams! Geronimo and his Apaches killed my parents, grandparents, and sister twenty years ago west of a town called Dead Horse on the Gila River."

Sutton, stunned, stared into Adams' brown eyes and then at his almost blond hair. "I was told you had brown hair, Adams."

"I did have brown hair when I was a boy. The sun has bleached it over the years. Who told you about me?"

Instead of answering, Sutton said, "Would you mind pulling up that tunic you're wearing?"

"What for?"

"Just do me a favor and indulge my curiosity."

Adams hesitated and then unbound the sash he wore around his waist and pulled up his tunic.

Sutton stared at the line of scar tissue crossing Adams' ribs. "Well, I'll be damned," he breathed. "I'd been told you'd somehow hurt yourself when you were a boy and that your ribs were scarred."

Sutton paused thoughtfully and then, "You said before,

Adams, that it wasn't the Mexicans the Apaches massacred up near the border that had got you so upset. I understand now that you're on the killing trail on account of what the Apaches did to your family. But what I don't understand the least little bit is what took you so long to get your dander up."

"I was taken captive by Geronimo. Did you know that too?"

Sutton nodded.

"I got away from them together with a woman named Annie Everett. She made it but I didn't. They caught me and brought me back. I bided my time. I'd been with the Apaches for a year when I escaped again and this time I did get away."

"You lived wild," Sutton interjected.

"A prospector caught me one day. His name was Matt Albright. He gentled me and I lived with him for a time but when he died I left his place and wound up in Phoenix —in the line for the soup kitchen that the Light of the Lord Mission was running there. I persuaded them to give me a job as a swamper. Not for money—for food and lodging.

"There was a Mr. and Mrs. Chandler running the mission then. They took me in and later gave me their last name. I took the name Wayne because Matt Albright used to talk about a town back East where he came from. It was named Wayne. I did it, you might say, in memory of Matt and because he had been so kind to me when I was nothing but a barbarian trying to survive in the wilderness."

"An eight-year-old barbarian," Sutton said softly. Then, "Adams, I still don't understand why you waited so long to get even with the Apaches."

"I remembered nothing about the massacre of my family. Not a thing through all these years. All of it was completely wiped from my memory. But then—"

"When you saw what the Apaches did to that Mexican family—"

"It all came rushing back to me," Adams said, interrupting Sutton. "It was as if it were happening all over again. I heard the screams. I saw what they did to that young woman. I tried to stop them but I couldn't. Luke, it was awful, horrible. I tried to save them. I did. I really did, Luke. You've got to believe me. I did my best but my best wasn't good enough. They're dead. They're all dead because of me."

Sutton let the breath he had not realized he had been holding sigh out from between his teeth. "You were seven years old, Adams. There wasn't anything you could have done."

"Seven years old? No. When those Mexicans—"

"I'm talking about the day your parents and grandparents were wiped out. You were only seven then. There was just no way you could have stopped what happened so there's no reason in the world for you to feel guilty about it. It wasn't your fault."

"It wasn't my—"

"It wasn't your fault," Sutton repeated firmly.

Adams glanced at Geronimo and then back at Sutton.

Sutton saw the tears form in Adams' eyes and his fists unclenched. He watched in silence as Adams wept just as he had wept following the knifing of the young Mexican woman. He looked up at Nelson and Petry who were sitting their horses with unreadable expressions on their faces and then went up to Adams and put an arm around the man's shoulder.

Adams looked tearfully at Sutton, unable to speak.

"Maybe you're wondering how come I know so much about you, Adams."

"How—" The one word was all Adams could manage.

"I've been trailing you. I was hired to trail you."

"Hired? Who hired you?"

"Your sister."

"My *sister?* But she was killed along with my parents and grandparents."

"I'm glad to tell you, Adams, that you're as wrong as can be about that. She's alive and living up in Virginia City, Nevada. She's missed you all these years and she's been wanting her brother back real bad. She hired me to see if I could find you if you were anywhere to be found. Well, it seems like I did. Find you, I mean. So now I reckon it's time you and me set out to see her. You two can have a real fine reunion together. A regular jamboree."

Sutton turned to Nelson. "Geronimo's all yours, Lieutenant. Adams here's mine. At least he is till I turn him over to his sister."

Nelson bent down and held out his hand.

Sutton left Adams and went over and shook the offered hand. "Lieutenant, you may be fresh out of West Point and you sure do have a whole helluva lot left to learn about the West and what goes on in it, but I can tell you true that I'm mighty glad I'm not an Apache with you on my backtrail. You're a persistent man, Lieutenant. And you sure do know how to lead a rip-roaring cavalry charge when you set your mind to it."

Nelson smiled and gripped Sutton's hand tighter. "I'm ready to admit that I do have a lot to learn, Luke. I only wish you were the one who could take the time and trouble to teach me but I'm aware that you have a far more pressing matter to attend to."

"I hope you and your boys'll have an easy time of it on your way back to the reservation, Lieutenant. Sergeant."

Both cavalrymen saluted Sutton and then, with Geronimo walking in front of their horses, they and the two troopers rode out of the draw.

Sutton turned to Adams. "It's a long way back to Virginia City. We'd best fix up that bad arm of yours as best we can and then get a move on."

Adams smiled. Nodded.

Later, with his wound covered by a piece of his torn tunic, he rode beside Sutton as both men made their way out of the draw.

"Luke, I'm scared," Adams said as he walked with Sutton through Virginia City wearing the clothes he had bought for himself in Yuma, the ones Sutton had told him made him look like "a tried and true townsman."

"Scared? Scared of what?"

"Ghosts."

"Don't follow you."

"When I see Edith again—when she sees me—we'll both remember what happened that day near Dead Horse. Maybe ghosts will come between us and make it hard for us to get along with or even to like each other very much. We'll remind each other all the time of what happened to our parents and grandparents—and to us afterward—even if we decide never to talk about it."

"Seems to me a man who could fight Apaches the way you did oughtn't to be afraid of a few ghosts. Besides they might never put in an appearance. You'll just have to wait and see, you and your sister. Getting to know one another again, talking over the good times you must have had as kids—it'll likely work out. Mostly on account of you've found one another again."

"I'm still scared."

"Somebody once said or wrote, I don't rightly know which, 'Of ten troubles you can see coming down the road, nine may never arrive.'"

They walked on and Sutton finally turned and said, "Don't hang back, Vernon. You've got to take this bull by the horns." Several minutes later, Sutton pointed. "That's it. That's your sister's house. Up there on the grade."

Adams halted, his face frozen, as he stared at the house.

Sutton gripped his arm and led him on. When they were standing outside the front door, he slapped Adams on the back and then knocked resolutely on the door.

"I'm coming!" Mrs. Soames called out from somewhere inside the house, her voice faint as it drifted through the open window next to the door.

When the door opened, Sutton touched the brim of his hat to her.

"Mr. Sutton!" she exclaimed before he could utter a word. "Did you—?" Her eyes darted to Adams who stood stiffly, hat in hand, beside Sutton.

"I did, Mrs. Soames."

Her hand rose, reached out. Her fingers came to rest on Adams' cheek. Tears welled in her eyes. "Vernon? Is it really you, Vernon?"

Adams' hand rose and came to rest, covering his sister's. "Edith." He swallowed hard.

Then her arms were around him and his were around her and they wept. Then their weeping turned to laughter, which bounded down off the porch and out into the yard as Vernon lifted his sister off her feet, spun her around, and eagerly kissed her several times.

"Did Mr. Sutton tell you how I came here?" Mrs. Soames asked, when Adams finally put her down and she held him out at arm's length so she could look him up and down. "That I was married? Widowed?"

"Yes, he did. But I made him promise not to tell you about some of the terrible—"

"Wonderful things he did down through the years," Sutton said sharply, drowning out the word "terrible." "But I'm about to break my promise. Make him tell you something about the years he spent working and doing good as a missionary among the Apaches."

"Among the Apaches?" Mrs. Soames asked, incredulous. "You didn't, Vernon! *Did* you?"

"He did, Mrs. Soames," Sutton said. "He saw to it that they got enough to eat on the reservation and that they weren't cheated by tricky men with cattle to sell—well, you be sure to make him tell you all about it sometime."

"Oh!" Mrs. Soames exclaimed. "Whatever am I thinking of? Come in, both of you, come along inside."

"Come on, Luke," Adams said before he and his sister entered the house together.

When Sutton remained outside, they both turned and smiling, beckoned to him.

He shook his head. "You two have a whole lot of catching up to do. I don't want to get in the way of that."

"Nonsense!" Mrs. Soames cried and hurried up to him. She took his arm but he stood his ground.

"I'll come by and visit the two of you sometime soon," he promised. "Once you've had a chance to settle down and get to know each other all over again."

"Luke," Adams began nervously, "don't—"

"I'll be leaving you now, Vernon, but before I do there's a question I want to put to you."

"A question?"

"First, let me have a private word with your sister here." Sutton bent over and whispered in Mrs. Soames's ear. When she eagerly nodded and cast a loving glance at her brother, he said, "Vernon, do you remember what a biscuit-eating boy you used to be?"

For a moment, Adams' face showed no sign of comprehension. But then, his face beaming, he said, "My mother used to make the best biscuits in the whole world, and oh, my, how I did dote on them. I can almost taste them this very minute."

"Well, then, I've got some good news to tell you, Vernon. Your sister still uses your ma's recipe when she bakes biscuits and she just agreed to fire up her oven right now and get out the flour and fixings."

"Of course, I must add a word of caution," Mrs. Soames said soberly, her eyes cast down.

"Is something wrong, Edith?" Adams asked, coming up to her.

"There may be. My biscuits, I confess, have never turned out as well as Ma's did."

Vernon laughed. He put his arm around his sister and hugged her. "Don't worry," he told her. "If your biscuits are even half as good as Ma's used to be, I'll eat a whole panful of them all by myself. That's a promise!"

"Some things never change, do they?" Mrs. Soames said and smiled broadly at her brother.

Sutton, unnoticed by either of them had stepped down off the porch and was walking away.

"Vernon," he heard Mrs. Soames behind him say, "my memory must be giving out on me. I could have sworn your hair was brown."

". . . done by the sun," Sutton heard Vernon say before the door closed behind him and his sister.

Sutton made his way down C Street, heading for the International Hotel, a bath, and a good hot meal in that order.

But as he was passing the iron-faced brick building that housed the *Territorial Enterprise*, he heard his name called.

A moment later Bill Wright dashed out of the building and began to pump Sutton's hand. "How did you make out, Luke?"

"Make out?"

"Did you find Vernon Adams?"

"You know about that matter, Bill?"

"Almost everyone in town knows about it. Mrs. Soames was so happy that you agreed to search for her brother—why, that's almost all she has talked about since the day you left town—and to just about anyone and everyone who would listen to her soaring hopes of seeing her brother again instilled in her, she told me personally, and these were her very own words, 'by that very persistent and resourceful man Mr. Luke Sutton.'"

Sutton grinned and briefly told Wright what had happened and how he had finally found Vernon Adams.

"Apparently there is just no stopping you once you set your mind to doing something, Luke," Wright commented. "Mrs. Soames was evidently right. You are a persistent man."

"Stubborn might be a better word for me, Bill. A fellow once said about me that I'm stubborn enough to butt heads with a bull to get where I want to go, and I reckon that fellow was probably right."

Wright gazed thoughtfully at Sutton for a moment and then pointed to the building next door. "If you were to set out after *him,* I have not the slightest doubt that you'd run him to ground sooner or later."

Sutton stared at the wanted poster Wright had pointed out which was nailed to the wooden wall of the building next door.

"Finding that murderer would be a paying proposition for you, Luke," Wright declared, watching Sutton carefully and smiling.

"You mean there's a reward out on the jasper?"

"One thousand dollars. It says so right there on the poster."

"That's a lot of money."

Wright gave Sutton a wink and then, after making him promise to meet him that night in the bar of the International Hotel for a drink, he reentered his office.

Sutton went up to stand in front of the poster. He thumbed his hat back on his head, thrust his hands into the back pockets of his jeans, and read it carefully.

Then he ripped it from the wall and pocketed it before heading for the International Hotel.

ABOUT THE AUTHOR

Leo P. Kelley has written more than a dozen novels, including five Luke Sutton books, and published many short stories in leading magazines. His suspense novel *Deadlocked!* was nominated for the Mystery Writers of America's Edgar Award.